False Start

Bev Pettersen

Published by Westerhall, 2025.

To My Family

CHAPTER ONE

Nikki Drake eased her hatchback to a stop outside the women's shelter, cutting the headlights before they drew attention. Fog thickened the pre-dawn air, transforming streetlights into hazy orbs. This neighborhood belonged in the shadows, perfect for women who needed to disappear.

Her latest client hugged herself in the passenger seat, knuckles white where she gripped the sleeves of her thin sweater. Another surveillance case gone sideways, though this one had ended better than some. The woman would be safe here, at least for now.

"They'll take good care of you," Nikki said. The shelter staff knew their business. No questions asked, no judgments made. Just clean beds and locked doors. "If your brother doesn't show up tomorrow," she added, "call me. And remember what we discussed. New phone, new passwords, new accounts. Everything starts fresh."

"Thank you. I couldn't have done this on my own." The woman's voice cracked. She swallowed hard and slipped from the car. The shelter's steel door opened with a whisper of well-oiled hinges then closed behind her hunched shoulders.

Nikki waited until the security light blinked green, signaling the locks had engaged. Another name added to her list of fresh starts that never quite felt like victories. Gunner's nose appeared between the seats, his breath warming her neck. She scratched behind his ears, grateful that he'd alerted to the woman's husband. Thanks to her partner's keen senses, they'd been able to lose the man before there was any more violence.

She checked her dashboard clock, wondering if she'd be able to catch the morning workouts at Santa Anita, specifically Conan's scheduled breeze. The San Felipe Stakes winner had become the talk of the racing world, and she was curious to see if the colt could maintain his surprising form heading into the Santa Anita Derby.

Her boyfriend Justin—an LAPD homicide detective who'd owned racehorses for a decade—had mentioned that the colt's time might be something special. Between his police schedule and her PI caseload, their shared interest in horses had become one of the few constants where their hectic lives reliably intersected.

The gray-washed streets of Arcadia stretched empty before them, traffic signals blinking yellow at deserted intersections. She passed the quiet hulk of the mall, its vast parking lot empty except for early-morning walkers circling the perimeter. Palm trees lined the boulevard, their fronds barely stirring in the heavy air. Even the 24-hour restaurants near the track looked sleepy, though light spilled from the kitchen of her favorite diner where cooks prepared for the morning rush.

Nikki's mind drifted to Conan's stunning performance in the San Felipe Stakes three weeks earlier. The racing press had dubbed it the upset of the season—a 30-1 longshot from a virtually unknown trainer defeating the heavy favorite by two lengths. And not just any favorite, but Wellington's million-dollar colt Desert Warrior. Thoroughbred Daily had called it "the clearest repudiation of conventional wisdom since Mine That Bird's Derby shocker."

No wonder everyone wanted to see his work this morning. If Conan showed the same brilliance, the Santa Anita Derby might become a genuine showdown rather than the coronation many had expected for Wellington's stable star. Still, there was an edge to the trackside anticipation—Wellington hadn't nicknamed the colt "Conan the Barbarian" for nothing. Despite his San Felipe victory, no one knew for certain if they would witness a fast workout or an impromptu rodeo. The horse's reputation for unpredictability only added to the morning's suspense.

The backside lay shrouded in fog when Nikki arrived, though regular railbirds were already gathered. No Justin yet—his last message said he was stuck in a meeting with his trainer, Tom Wells, and would meet her at the barn.

She positioned herself twenty feet from the rail, sipping coffee while Gunner sat obediently at her feet. From this distance, her big Shepherd wouldn't spook the Thoroughbreds and she'd still be able to see the horses coming off the track.

"Shame Wellington's not here to see this," a gravelly voice said to her right. Nikki recognized the speaker—an aging exercise rider known for his unfiltered commentary. "Though maybe that's for the best."

"Why's that?" his companion asked.

"He's been on the warpath since the San Felipe. Can't believe a four-million-dollar purchase got beat by a colt he advised his Saudi owners to dump."

"That new trainer better be careful. Wellington doesn't like being embarrassed."

"Rachel Parker? Yeah, heard she used to gallop for him years back. Rumor is he fired her when she suggested one of his horses needed more ground training. Bad blood there, for sure."

Their conversation shifted to other topics, but Nikki filed away the information. The Santa Anita Derby loomed just two weeks away, and while interest always ran high, this morning's buzz felt different. The crowd was focused on one colt in particular, Conan, their anticipation evident in the media presence. But beneath the excitement ran an undercurrent of wariness and judgment.

"There he is," someone whispered as a dark bay horse emerged from the fog. Nikki straightened, eager for her first look at the San Felipe winner. She'd missed Conan's actual work but she'd get a good view when he walked off the track.

Her first impression was surprise. Conan approached the gap in the rail with relaxed grace. His neck was arched but his eye was calm and interested. He looked mentally healthy, content with his place in the world. One ear kept flicking back, attentive to his young rider who guided him off the track, a delighted smile curving her face.

After reading so much about the Cinderella story and how Parker had transformed Wellington's reject into a stakes winner, Nikki had expected something more visibly dramatic.

"Five-eighths in fifty-eight and change," an authoritative voice said. "Finished strong, galloped out three-quarters in one-eleven."

Appreciative murmurs rippled from the gathered horsemen. Little wonder the exercise rider looked happy. For a horse to break a minute for five furlongs while working in hand was impressive enough. But to gallop out another furlong in thirteen seconds showed natural speed and stamina, both required for the Derby's grueling distance. These weren't just good times. They were the kind of times one would expect from established winners, not a horse that Wellington, Conan's previous trainer, had dismissed as unmanageable.

A wiry groom stepped forward and attached a leather line to Conan's bridle, stroking the horse's neck before leading him away. Unlike other Derby hopefuls, Conan didn't have much of an entourage. Only his trainer, Rachel Parker, turned to follow the horse.

Nikki gave Rachel a respectful nod as the trainer passed. Everyone loved an underdog, and it appeared that Conan was a legitimate favorite. The Santa Anita Derby was shaping up to be a competitive race. It would be a boost for racing if a female trainer won, and even more exciting if Conan qualified for the Kentucky Derby.

A woman trainer had never won that race, nor had it ever been done by a trainer with a one-horse stable. Nikki found herself smiling at the thought of Rachel Parker making history, imagining headlines celebrating the tiny operation that toppled racing's male-dominated establishment. She'd always supported women pushing into traditionally male spaces. PI work had taught her how much harder they often had to work for the same recognition.

But as she walked behind Rachel, she noted a wariness in the woman's quick stride—the look of someone expecting trouble. Rachel's history certainly wasn't typical for someone handling a Derby contender: small-time trainer, cheap claiming horses, forced to use her teenage daughter as an exercise rider when no one else would risk going near the notorious colt.

Steps pounded behind her. Gunner twisted, bumping her leg as a tall, silver-haired man rushed past.

"It's okay, boy," she murmured, relieved that her dog's defensive movement was his only reaction.

When Justin had first bought Gunner from the K9 School and given him to Nikki, he would have considered the strange man a threat, and growled a warning. Although the man who'd just charged past wasn't really a stranger.

James Wellington III was one of the most recognizable figures on the North American race circuit. His illustrious family had championed racing integrity for generations and was credited with many backside initiatives. Their foundation funded everything from backstretch medical clinics to college scholarships for stable workers' children.

Wellington was in an obvious rush. Several onlookers exchanged knowing glances, as if they'd been expecting this confrontation. Nikki recalled the exercise rider's comments about "bad blood" between Wellington and Parker. Likely Wellington's appearance moments after Conan's impressive workout wasn't coincidental.

Rachel seemed oblivious to Wellington's presence until he grabbed her arm and yanked her to a stop. Nikki's eyes widened. She'd heard whispers about his temper—stories she'd always dismissed as competitors' jealousy or exaggeration. In her limited interactions with him at charity events, he'd epitomized the gentleman horseman, his polished manners as carefully cultivated as his tasteful clothes. But the man before her, face contorted with rage, bore little resemblance to that public image. This was the Wellington she'd never believed existed—until now.

"What the hell are you giving that horse?" he sputtered, so furious drops of spit flew from his mouth. "You have to be using drugs. There's no way he could change. No way!"

The morning fog had burned away, leaving the confrontation starkly visible in the strengthening light. Two exercise riders pulled up their horses, exchanging knowing glances as they watched the scene unfold. A groom paused with wheelbarrow suspended mid-dump. At a nearby barn, a trainer wearing a faded ball cap and his farrier turned, straining to catch every word.

"Let go of me." Rachel jerked her arm away. "You should be happy for the horse. It's not my fault your assessment of him was so short sighted."

Nikki tightened her grip on Gunner's leash. She didn't want to eavesdrop and Rachel didn't appear to need help. Horse people were tough, the women doubly so. But Wellington was leaning into Rachel's space with unusual aggression.

"You have to be using drugs," Wellington said, his voice carrying over the still air. "If this gets out on the Derby stage, do you even understand the impact? The sport is already suffering. And I'm not going to let you ruin what used to be a respected industry."

"That sounds like a threat," Rachel said.

"Yes, it is."

"I'm not a cheater." Rachel's cheeks flamed with color. "And just because Saudi sheiks send you their expensive horses doesn't mean you can control the winner's circle."

"Just watch what we control." Wellington glanced around, as if suddenly aware of his audience. Then he gave a contemptuous snort and strode away, leaving behind a brittle tension that crackled in his wake.

For a moment, Rachel's haunted gaze held Nikki's. Then she gave a little shrug, turned and trudged after her horse.

"Well, that was something," the nearby trainer muttered. "Haven't seen Wellington lose his cool for a while."

"Man's under pressure," the farrier replied. "His Saudi owners spent four million on Desert Warrior. They can't be happy watching Conan win, especially after Wellington convinced them to dump him."

"But he usually keeps his hands clean. Sends those lackeys to park outside rival barns, taking photos, watching who comes and goes. Remember what happened to Diaz before the Malibu Stakes? Poor trainer was so intimidated he scratched. And no one could pin anything on Wellington."

"Yeah, but this is different," the farrier said, expertly flipping a rasp in his big hand. "Those Saudi clients don't accept excuses, let alone failure. Billions in oil money buys a certain expectation. Who knows what they said to him after the San Felipe? For a man who's built his reputation on delivering winners, losing to his own cast-off must feel like career suicide. I wouldn't want to be in Wellington's shoes if he has to defend another loss."

The two men turned silent when they realized Nikki was within earshot. Around her, the morning routine resumed. The two exercise riders turned their horses away, the groom straightened his wheelbarrow and everyone avoided eye contact. The collective message was clear: conversations about Wellington were not for outsiders. Clearly the man had power.

Nikki continued walking, her body taut as she considered Wellington's outburst. Something about his intensity suggested more than wounded pride—a genuine fear that went beyond professional rivalry. Justin might know; he had more experience with the major players.

The familiar smells of hay, leather, and liniment pulled her forward, tension draining with each step closer to the barn. Justin stood outside the trainer's office, tall, athletic and imposing. Just the sight of him loosened the final knot between her shoulder blades.

"Heard about Conan's workout this morning. Impressive time," Justin said, admiration warming his voice. Then his expression shifted, becoming unreadable as he held out his phone. "But look at this."

The knot of tension returned as Nikki scanned the text. *Warning to all horsemen: Unqualified trainer using illegal substances on Derby contender. Test results pending. Public scandal imminent. Protect our sport!*

"Wellington works amazingly fast," she said, updating Justin on what she'd witnessed.

"Word is that he's terrified of his Saudi owners." Justin palmed his phone with a shake of his head. "Their horses represent millions in training fees and potential breeding rights. I've seen him destroy careers with a single phone call when his reputation is on the line."

Even as they spoke, two trainers hurried past, heads ducked in conversation. Further down the aisle, an exercise rider snatched up her beeping phone, though Nikki noticed she took time to smile at Justin first.

"Once drug whispers start," Justin said, his voice lowering, "it means blood tests, barn searches, feed testing. One mistake with medications could end her career. Brutal for any trainer. Worse for an outsider like Rachel Parker."

"And Wellington's connected to officials," Nikki said. "She might not even know what's going on. I should warn her."

"Thought you'd feel that way." Justin gave a resigned smile, his hand brushing her shoulder in both a caress and a warning. "Remember, Wellington can be ruthless when he thinks he's right."

"I wonder who else received this message," Nikki said, already calculating the damage that might be spreading.

"Probably every trainer, owner, and racing official with Santa Anita credentials," Justin said. "Minus Rachel Parker. I'll have tech trace the text for you. See if they can identify the source."

Nikki gave him a grateful smile. Justin was a top detective with access to information that her one-person office didn't enjoy. His backing of Rachel wasn't surprising. He'd always helped the underdog, even when he was a university student providing Nikki and her sister with free riding lessons.

A horse whinnied from a nearby stall, the sound jarring against their solemn discussion. But it was a reminder that beneath all the power plays, this was still about horses. About a small-time trainer who'd somehow transformed a rejected colt into a Derby contender. The kind of story that should be celebrated, not destroyed.

"I'll go find Rachel now," Nikki said, setting her jaw and shortening Gunner's leash. Conan and his trainer had earned their shot, and she wasn't about to let Wellington's influence crush them before Rachel had the chance to mount a defense.

Justin's phone buzzed, probably his homicide case calling. He'd been juggling a complex investigation all week, catching sleep between witness interviews and crime scene processing. "Just be careful, Nik," he said, before taking the call.

Nikki nodded. She only planned to warn Rachel about Wellington's text. Simple enough. But something in Justin's grim expression made her wonder if anything involving horses and powerful men was ever simple.

CHAPTER TWO

Nikki strode toward the far end of Santa Anita's backside, passing tidy shedrows where horses dozed contentedly in front of cooling fans. The San Gabriel Mountains loomed above the barns, their peaks sharp against the morning sky. It was just past nine, late enough that most horses had already completed their morning works. And she already knew Conan had headed back to his barn.

The steady rhythm of mechanical hotwalkers mixed with the scent of hay and sweet feed. She passed trainers checking legs and grooms bathing horses, methodically working through morning chores. The peaceful routine felt at odds with the knowledge of Wellington's smear campaign.

Nikki glanced left and right, hoping to spot Conan, unsure where to find his barn. She asked a few workers but only received nervous shrugs. Their reactions told her Wellington's influence was already at work. No one wanted to be seen helping Rachel Parker.

Finally, an elderly groom pointed her way. "Lady with the big horse? She rents from Pete Jackson. Past maintenance, near the old hay barn." His kind gaze held hers for a moment, before turning back to hanging dripping bandages on a wash line.

The location fit Rachel's outsider status. Pete Jackson trained claiming horses, his operation less visible among the powerhouse stables that dominated racing headlines. Not where you'd expect to find a Derby contender.

Nikki rounded the maintenance building and immediately spotted Conan. Even at this distance, his presence commanded attention. The strapping bay stood like royalty while his groom checked his legs, the man more concerned with post-workout protocol than the horse's notorious teeth. The groom's careful movements showed both professional pride and genuine affection for his charge.

"Si, Kat," he said to a teenager lugging two sloshing water buckets. "He can have another drink. But not too much."

Nikki absorbed the scene. If rumors were true, Kat was Rachel's daughter, hence both her riding and barn duties. Neither she nor the groom showed any fear of the horse. Their movements were calm and practiced, treating him like any other Thoroughbred.

Conan noticed her first, his head lifting with interest. Nikki kept Gunner close, though her dog was great with livestock and well used to horses. It was notable that the Shepherd's relaxed posture showed he sensed no threat from the colt.

Kat turned, following the direction of Conan's pricked ears. Her smile faded. "Like I told the others," she said, voice weary beyond her years, "we aren't giving interviews. Not today."

"I'm not press," Nikki said, studying the girl's protective stance. The wariness made sense. Every media report she'd seen had twisted their words, amplifying Wellington's claims about Conan being dangerous. After having their statements repeatedly distorted and turned against them, this family had learned to be cautious around strangers. "I just need to talk to Rachel Parker. Is she your mom?"

The girl's guarded gaze flickered toward the shedrow. Rachel watched from the entrance. Even in worn jeans and a faded work shirt, she had a natural grace. Her dark hair was pulled back in a casual ponytail that emphasized high cheekbones and striking green eyes—the kind of effortless beauty that seemed undiminished by the stress of training.

"Hi, Rachel." Nikki stepped closer and offered her business card. "I saw you by the gap this morning."

"I remember. Hard to forget such a well-behaved dog." Rachel's gaze stayed on Nikki rather than her PI credentials. "You're Nikki Drake, aren't you? The PI who found the kitchen worker's son." Her expression warmed. "And you're with Justin Decker. His reputation with horsemen is solid. If you'd been here ten minutes earlier, you could have helped chase off the media. Wellington is really stirring things up."

Nikki caught the frustration in Rachel's voice. "The text? You've seen it?"

"Yes, but it's no problem. That drug charge is totally unfounded." Rachel lifted her chin, the same way she'd reacted to Wellington's verbal threat. Her shoulders squared, posture straightening as if physically bracing. "Conan gets hay and oats, that's all. But my lawyer says we can't prove libel without identifying the source. And Wellington's too smart for that. But it's no problem," she repeated.

Her forced bravado didn't match the way her hands clenched, small betrayals of the fear she tried to mask. This woman had turned a castoff horse into something remarkable, only to have it threatened by a man with unlimited resources. The unfairness strengthened Nikki's resolve to help, even though Rachel was trying to pretend she didn't need assistance.

Footsteps shuffled in the aisle. A gray-haired man emerged, his manner deferential but determined. Pete Jackson—the man whose name wasn't even posted on his own barn.

"Actually, there is a problem," Jackson said, his eyes darting everywhere but at Rachel. "With these drug rumors, I can't risk having your horse here. My owners are calling. Getting jumpy."

Rachel jerked back, arms dropping to her sides as if she'd been struck. "You're evicting us? Now? Two weeks before the big race?"

"You have to understand." Jackson's voice turned pleading. "My stable can't afford the scandal. And Wellington called…" He caught himself, mouth snapping shut before he scurried away.

Nikki noted his hasty retreat, the way he looked over his shoulder, not wanting to be seen helping the wrong side. Every trainer on the backside lived one bad day from disaster. One failed drug test, one scandal, and years of hard work could vanish overnight. Wellington knew how to apply pressure.

Rachel leaned against the barn door, dismay etching lines around her mouth. In the racing world, stall space was like gold. Without it, you couldn't train. Without training, you couldn't earn. The brutal math was inescapable.

"It's okay, Mom," Kat said, rushing to her mother's side, all teenage defiance. "Conan's already familiar with this track. Besides, he likes Mountain View way better than this dump."

Her middle finger punctuated the sentiment in Jackson's direction. But Nikki caught the worry in Rachel's eyes. A public training center meant less security, more exposure, more challenges.

"Do you have any other options for stalls?" Nikki asked, mentally reviewing local facilities.

"A few." Rachel rubbed her forehead. "But Mountain View has the best track. And Conan really does love it there. Although the security is different than here."

Their gazes met, sharing silent understanding of the risk.

"Maybe I should hire you," Rachel said slowly. "Just for half a day? Would you follow my groom, Marco, and me out this afternoon? Check the security setup?"

Nikki pressed her lips together. Rachel Parker had transformed a rebellious horse into a Derby contender with nothing but a teenage exercise rider and a loyal groom. The racing establishment should be helpful. Instead, they were closing ranks. A woman trainer with no connections and a horse Wellington had tossed aside—their very existence challenged the power structure.

The groom moved closer. Marco was also invested in Conan's care. And he didn't seem worried about the horse's behavior. He wasn't even using a stud chain on the halter. And that was the only thing making Nikki hesitate: that Conan might hurt someone. Of course, much of the horse's rep seemed unfounded.

"I'll help," she said. "No charge until he runs in the Derby."

Kat's smile lit up her face, her reserve melting. She dropped to scratch Gunner's ears, laughing when he offered his paw. "I've got to get to school. But I know your big dog can keep those bullies away!"

The normalcy of it hit Nikki hard—a high school girl worried about both homework and harassment, a mother trying to protect their family dream, a small team who'd dared to prove the experts wrong. They'd created something special. And sadly that had made them targets.

As Kat hurried away, Nikki caught Rachel's tight smile. The trainer knew exactly what she faced. Wellington hadn't just been wrong about Conan. He'd been wrong in front of the entire racing world, including his Saudi owners. For a man like Wellington, that might be unforgiveable.

CHAPTER THREE

Nikki followed the horse trailer onto the dirt road to Mountain View Training Center, staying well back from the belching exhaust. The rusty trailer ahead of her bounced on worn springs, its red paint bleached to a dull pink. A pothole sent it lurching violently, the jolt transferring to its equine passenger. Unlike humans who could brace against sudden movements, horses couldn't grip. Their legs absorbed every bump. A punishing ride could leave muscles sore and tendons strained.

Wellington had forced Rachel to move Conan from a secured track to this remote facility. And he'd made sure the colt had a rough ride. In another of his power moves, Rachel's regular shipper had refused service, citing sudden insurance issues.

Nikki pulled her worried gaze off the trailer and began assessing the center's vulnerabilities: the public road running past weathered barns, no perimeter fence and no obvious security guard. The road on the far side of the track, probably meant for hikers accessing the mountain trails, also offered easy entry.

She parked beside Rachel's battered truck, near the end barn, its exposed location confirming her security fears. Unlike the central barns, tucked beside the office and grandstand, this isolated building was vulnerable from three sides. Its rear door backed onto a horse path where anyone could approach, while the other end opened directly to the road. Exterior lighting consisted of one lamp over the end door.

Marco seemed oblivious, just relieved to lead Conan off the rusty trailer and onto safe ground. Two horses called a welcome, and Conan gave a shrill nicker as he walked eagerly beside Marco and into the barn.

Conan looked sound, unfazed by his bumpy ride. And this confident, well-mannered colt bore no resemblance to rumors of an unmanageable savage. Either Wellington had been spectacularly wrong, or Conan's behavior had changed.

Nikki moved closer to the trailer as the driver handed Rachel the shipping papers. "I can't haul him back for you," he said. "Just landed an unexpected contract through the end of the month. Have to take it. You might try someone out of state."

"No problem," Rachel said, but Nikki noticed her hand shook as she signed the document and jammed a copy into her rear pocket. The driver leaned closer, voice dropping.

I shouldn't say this, but..." He glanced nervously over his shoulder. "Got calls from three different people yesterday. Asking if I was hauling for you, when exactly, what route. Never had that happen before."

Nikki and Rachel exchanged glances, the implications clear. Wellington had found Conan already.

"Thank you," Nikki said to the driver. "For the warning."

Rachel gave him a short nod then hurried into the barn. Nikki followed more slowly, walking the aisle and pressing notes into her phone. Gunner moved beside her, nose cataloging the various scents.

When he veered into the open feed room and lunged between grain bins, his lightning strike eliminated one rat, but highlighted another vulnerability. The feed room's broken lock meant anyone could tamper with Conan's food.

Marco grabbed a shovel, eyeing the dog with growing respect. "Not bad," he said, clearly impressed by Gunner's speed.

Nikki praised Gunner then told him to leave it, stepping back so Marco could scoop up the rodent. She made a few more notations then walked back down the aisle and joined Rachel.

A hiker with a bright orange backpack looked in and called a cheerful greeting as he strode by the barn.

Rachel barely looked up from filling Conan's hay nets—two identical ones she hung side by side. There were also two white salt blocks mounted at the same height on the wall. Just extra food to watch, Nikki thought, but right now, after seeing the hiker, her bigger concern was about unchallenged visitors.

"Do people cut through here often?"

"A few," Rachel said. "It's a public access road."

"At least there's surveillance," Nikki said, eyeing the security camera above the end door.

"No, there isn't," Marco said, stopping beside her and setting down the wheelbarrow. His earlier reserve had disappeared and he kept peering at Gunner, as if hoping to see him grab another rat.

"Those cameras are only for show," Rachel added. "But there's never much traffic. The main road to the trailhead is on the other side of the track. Most hikers use that."

Nikki's mouth tightened as she moved to the barn door, checking sight lines. The facility owner's house sat at the far end of the property, a one-story building with a partial view of the barns. Close enough to hear a ruckus. Too far to spot someone slipping something into a feed bucket.

For a horse though, this place was heaven with its open spaces, private paddocks and green grass. Away from the loudspeakers and compressed quarters of Santa Anita, a high-strung Thoroughbred could truly relax.

She walked back to Rachel. "I can understand why Conan prefers it here. Is this where his behavior improved?"

"Let's focus on security," Rachel said, turning away and fiddling with the stall latch. "That's what's important."

Nikki noted her deflection with a twinge of alarm. A horse's dramatic turnaround was usually a trainer's favorite topic. They'd talk for hours about feed changes, training techniques, the moment everything clicked. But Rachel had just shut down at the mention of Conan's transformation. That kind of reluctance often stemmed from either guilt or fear.

"You need working cameras," Nikki said, pushing aside her concerns. "My contact can install them quickly. But Conan also needs 24-hour human surveillance."

"We can do that," Rachel said. "Kat will come before school to ride. And I'll be here early morning to sunset. Marco has already offered to sleep in the afternoons and watch Conan at night."

"Good. And check the paddock every time before turning him out. Do you know the other people and horses in this barn? Or do they change often?"

"I know them all. I've been training out of here for years. There's not much turnover."

Rachel's attention shifted, caught by a car crawling along the public road. Much too slow for a passerby heading for a hike. Gunner also tracked its movement, ears pricked. The vehicle slowed even more, inching past the barn entrance, engine nearly silent.

"Biggest priority is securing feed and water," Nikki said, continuing her security assessment while keeping an eye on the car. "Times, amounts, who handles it. And no sharing of buckets or brushes. Everything Conan consumes needs documentation."

"We already do—" Rachel's words cut off as another vehicle approached, this one a dark Ford Explorer. It idled a mere thirty feet from the barn, remaining for long seconds before accelerating away, its tires spraying dirt as it spun over the edge of the flower bed.

"And I mean everything." Nikki spoke through tight lips. "Shampoos, liniments, even fly spray. You'll need fresh bottles, sealed and dated." She held up a well-used jar of liniment from the tack room shelf. "This needs to go."

Rachel and Marco were trying to listen, but their attention kept jumping to the road, as if puzzled by the unusual traffic. When a beige sedan rolled past, matching the others' predatory pace, Nikki charged out. These weren't casual observers. This was coordinated surveillance, intended to disrupt. Or frighten.

She raised her phone to snap a picture, but the car accelerated, dust obscuring its plate. This matched what she'd heard about Wellington's tactics. Justin had warned her that his polished manners disappeared when the stakes were high. The man's threat rang in her ears: "Just watch what we control."

She strode back into the barn, keeping her voice steady despite her anger. Her initial half-day agreement suddenly seemed inadequate. These people needed real protection, and she wasn't about to abandon them when the threats were just beginning to materialize.

"Everything gets replaced," she said. "Everything gets locked up. And no one—no one—leaves Conan unattended."

Marco and Rachel exchanged a silent look as understanding dawned. Wellington's people weren't just watching. They were announcing their presence. And that sort of boldness often escalated into something far more dangerous.

CHAPTER FOUR

Nikki climbed the narrow stairs to her second-floor office, breathing in the smell of Vinny's garlic bread from the nearby restaurant. The worn steps creaked under her feet, each sound as familiar as an old friend. Perfect location really—quick parking in back, patch of grass for Gunner, and the kind of neighbors who noticed everything but minded their own business. Best of all, her friend Sonja rented the adjacent office.

She unlocked her door and went straight to the equipment cabinet, pulling out surveillance gear. Mini cameras, motion sensors, hotspots—everything needed to monitor Mountain View's vulnerabilities. Rachel would focus her limited funds on Conan's stall, but that access road was an invitation to trouble. Coverage was essential.

Gunner's nails clicked against the worn linoleum as he inspected the familiar space. She could afford fancier digs now, maybe even one of those gleaming downtown offices with a prestigious address. But this shabby strip of tattoo parlors and consignment shops had become home.

Like the racing backside, the real stories happened in places that weren't too polished. She was happy she'd signed another year's lease, despite the upgrading suggested by her accountant. The rent was reasonable, the small-business neighbors were better than any security system, and Vinny kept Gunner supplied with fresh-baked dog biscuits.

Her phone buzzed as she placed the camera in her pack. Mike Jensen's name caught her eye—an acquaintance, and a veteran turf writer whose blog carried serious weight in racing circles. His reputation for uncovering scandals had upended more than one training career. She scanned the headline, her stomach clenching.

SANTA ANITA SENSATION? OR SCANDAL? By Mike Jensen, Racing Insider Blog

The fairy tale story of Conan's rise from track terror to Derby contender is raising eyebrows in racing circles. The colt's dramatic transformation under small-time trainer Rachel Parker has veterans questioning what's behind this "miracle."

Leading trainer James Wellington III, who previously handled the horse, expressed concerns about unexplainable behavioral changes that defy normal training progression. Wellington, whose family has championed racing integrity for three generations, warns that such sudden improvements often have darker explanations.

"In forty years, I've never seen a truly dangerous horse turn around this quickly without chemical assistance," says one prominent California trainer who wished to remain anonymous. "The racing community needs to protect its integrity."

Parker, who has never trained a stakes horse, keeps Conan at an off-track facility, away from regular testing protocols. Sources say track officials are investigating, but declined to comment on specific allegations.

With the Santa Anita Derby only nine days away, the question remains: Is this a Cinderella story, or another black eye for a sport struggling with its image?

Nikki groaned and headed straight to Sonja's office. If anyone understood mysterious transformations in horses, it would be her friend. Besides, she wanted to process what she'd just witnessed at Mountain View.

The door opened before she could knock. Sonja stood smiling, blonde braid over her shoulder, flowing skirt brushing her colorful sandals. The brown pit bull beside her, Ginger, greeted them with wagging tail and bright eyes, quite a transformation from the neglected dog who'd helped Nikki survive a recent drug case. Ginger licked Gunner's face in respectful greeting, her gentle demeanor a testament to Sonja's healing touch.

"They just finalized Ginger's paperwork. I officially own her now!" Sonja wrapped Nikki in a grateful hug then settled in her wicker chair, the one she'd used for countless psychic sessions before discovering her gift for animal communication.

"It's been over a week since I made it to the track," Sonja went on, her smile turning rueful. "But I saw media reports about the new Derby favorite. The racing world can be cruel to outsiders. Especially women who don't fit the traditional mold."

"You've heard about Rachel Parker and Conan?" Nikki wasn't really surprised. Sonja always seemed to know things before they happened. The shelves behind her held a curious mix. Incense alongside racing trophies, and tarot cards next to framed winner's circle photos. Sonja had found her niche bridging racing's pragmatic and spiritual worlds.

"Conan looks happy and healthy," Nikki went on. "Rachel documents everything—feed, medications, exercise. But mention his transformation, and she practically runs away. That kind of selective transparency worries me."

"Traditional trainers don't always appreciate alternative approaches. Maybe she has reasons for staying quiet." Something in Sonja's voice made Nikki look closer. Her friend was arranging crystals on her desk with unusual precision.

"But Wellington's not just spreading rumors," Nikki said. "He's trying to destroy her career."

"People like that can't stand being wrong." Sonja's fingers traced a crystal's purple edges. "Their reputation depends on being the expert, the one who knows best. But horses know who really understands them."

"Conan seems to be doing well. No longer dangerous."

"Maybe he never was. Or is that just what everyone assumed because he was so precocious?" Sonja glanced up, eyes sharp despite her reflective tone. "Sometimes we see what we expect to see. Wellington expected a rebel, so that's what he got. Rachel expected better, and Conan lived up to that too."

"You sound like you know something specific?" Nikki waited an inviting moment but Sonja didn't answer. "I just wish Rachel would be more open," Nikki added. "The avoidance makes her look guilty, as if she *is* using drugs."

"Sometimes the simplest explanation isn't chemical." Sonja twisted her braid. "Some horses just need more time and understanding."

Something about her careful phrasing made Nikki pause. She often bounced cases off her friend but if Sonja knew more, she wasn't ready to share.

"I'm meeting Justin for dinner," Nikki said, watching Sonja's reaction. "He might know more about the drug testing angle."

"Better hurry then." Sonja turned away, busying herself with arranging incense candles. Her braid swung like a pendulum as she moved items with unnecessary attention, signaling the conversation was over.

Nikki rose, caught off guard by her friend's abrupt shift. Sonja, who could talk for hours about horse psychology, was suddenly too absorbed in aligning candles to meet her eyes. The dismissal felt almost defensive.

She returned to her office and grabbed her phone before descending to the street. Vinny's patio glowed with warm light, and delicious aromas wafted through the evening air. However, her appetite had faded. First Rachel's evasiveness, now Sonja's reluctance. It left her uneasy.

Justin looked up from their corner table, his eyes narrowing. "Something on your mind?" He pulled out her chair, avoiding the water bowl and dog biscuits waiting beneath the table, Vinny's standing order since Gunner had prevented a robbery there two years ago.

She showed Justin the blog article. "Wellington's definitely orchestrating a smear campaign. No direct accusations, just spreading doubt. And Rachel's making it easy for him."

"Tech couldn't trace that text," Justin said as their usual order arrived. Linguine with clams for him and, for Nikki, chicken marsala. Steam rose from the plates, carrying hints of wine and garlic.

"Burner phone," he added. "Long gone. But timing's interesting, right after Conan showed his speed."

"Seems as if Wellington was waiting to see if he was a genuine threat." Nikki pushed her food around, feeling disloyal to her client for bringing it up. "What about calming drugs?" she asked. "The kind that might stay in his system for months?"

Justin's fork stilled. "There are a few. Any vet could prescribe them. You think Rachel used them?"

"I don't know what to think. Something changed that horse. And Rachel is hiding something. Even Sonja shut me down when I mentioned it." Nikki described what she'd seen at Mountain View, along with the way Rachel avoided direct answers.

"Want me to run Rachel's background?" When Nikki hesitated, he added, "You always protect your clients, Nik. But let's make sure you know who you're protecting. And why."

A burst of laughter from nearby diners made her glance sideways. Normal people enjoying a normal evening, while she wrestled with growing suspicions about her client.

She blew out a sigh. "But I've seen them with the horse. They're clearly devoted. What if Rachel did use something months ago, and it cleared his system? That's not exactly a crime."

"It could be. Those tests detect nanograms. If she used anything illegal, Wellington won't stop until he finds it." Candlelight caught Justin's face, highlighting the concern in his dark eyes. Sometimes she forgot he'd seen firsthand how ugly racing politics could get, how careers could be destroyed.

"Tomorrow I'll do a deep dive at Mountain View," she said, squaring her shoulders. "Wellington's pressing hard and Rachel's not talking. It's time to find out what she's protecting."

Justin set down his fork. They both knew that once she committed to uncovering the truth, especially when it involved someone vulnerable, nothing would stop her. Not even Wellington's powerful reach.

"Be careful," he said, reaching across to touch her hand. "Sometimes people have good reasons for keeping secrets. And sometimes those secrets can get people killed."

CHAPTER FIVE

Pink tinted the skyline as Nikki turned onto Mountain View's deserted drive. After yesterday's hostile traffic, the early morning peace was a relief. She parked her car and opened the door for Gunner, noting the flowerbed bordering the road. The bougainvillea swayed in the breeze, their blooms offering both a cheery welcome and an excellent spot to hide a camera.

The sweet smell of alfalfa greeted her when she entered the barn. Grooms moved efficiently, scrubbing water buckets, grooming horses and gathering tack. She peered into Conan's empty stall where Marco was spreading fresh straw.

"Conan's headed for the track," he said.

She nodded her thanks, automatically studying the stall setup. The matching haynets and double salt blocks still seemed strange. But it was clear Marco was keeping a good eye on both the stall and attached paddock. His gaze swept continuously between the stall and the paddock. There'd be no chance of anyone tossing something over the fence or through the stall bars while he was on duty.

Nikki left the barn through the rear door with Gunner by her side. The dirt path led directly to the track and was wide and well maintained, providing good footing for horses. She joined Rachel beside the gap, noting how curious observers had already gathered. Word about Wellington's accusations had spread fast. She recognized one trainer who normally wouldn't drive from Santa Anita this early, merely to watch a rival gallop.

Kat was guiding Conan counter clockwise along the outer rail, his stride smooth and even. His dark coat gleamed, muscles rippling under the strengthening sun. His neck was bowed but he remained responsive to his rider's hold, not fighting but definitely keen to stretch out.

"Love how he waits on his rider," a horseman commented to his companion. "Mark of good training."

Nikki glanced at Rachel, hoping she'd heard the compliment. The woman needed to know that not everyone was against her. But Rachel stared straight ahead, watching as Kat let Conan stretch into an easy gallop.

His motion was almost hypnotic, powerful yet perfectly balanced. None of Wellington's stories about a fractious outlaw showed in his fluid movement, or in Kat's relaxed handling. A red-tailed hawk lifted from a rail post, its cry piercing the dawn quiet. But Conan never flinched, focused on his job.

When they trotted back to the gap, he wasn't even breathing hard. Kat calmly walked him off the track and toward the barn as if he'd never had a difficult day in his life.

Nikki fell into step beside Rachel as they followed horse and rider along the path. "You can breathe now," she said, noticing how Rachel's shoulders had finally relaxed.

"Was I that obvious?" Rachel's laugh held traces of leftover tension. "But he stayed nice and calm, exactly what we needed after yesterday's work."

They entered the barn just as Kat stopped Conan in the aisle. She shot Nikki a big smile then dismounted, giving Conan's neck an affectionate pat before Marco led him away to cool out. Her movements showed the easy confidence of someone raised around horses, a stark contrast to her guarded behavior around people.

"You two looked good out there," Nikki said. "You must have been on horses since you could walk."

"Yes, Mom taught me everything." The teen's face lit up at the safe topic. "I love developing young horses. It would be better if our jockey, Elena, could be on him for his final work, but she's confident after the San Felipe win. She'll fly in for the Derby."

Kat knelt to scratch Gunner's chest, laughing when he rolled over, a trust he rarely showed strangers. "Yesterday was scary though," she went on, still smiling up at Nikki. "You two really helped. I'm glad you're here."

She gave Gunner a last scratch then reluctantly rose. "Gotta get to school."

She hurried out the door, her steps light. Today, everything seemed right in her world. But she glanced around on her way out, as if checking for reporters. Not surprising. They certainly hadn't been kind.

"You like her too, don't you," Nikki said to Gunner before heading to the side of the barn where Marco and Rachel were cooling out Conan. Rachel had filled two water buckets while Marco walked him in circles, both of them murmuring praise, treating him exactly as they had yesterday at Santa Anita. The colt soaked up their attention like a pampered celebrity, as if expecting nothing less.

Suddenly both he and Gunner turned, their ears pricked toward the sound of an approaching vehicle. Nikki tensed, yesterday's threatening parade fresh in her mind. Seconds later, she relaxed, realizing it was only the surveillance contractor arriving in a van plastered with his company logo.

Nikki and Rachel walked out to meet him as he gathered equipment from his van, tablet in hand.

Rachel led him through the barn, stopping in front of Conan's stall. Her arms swept wide as she explained their security needs. Their voices drifted down the aisle—packages, monthly rates, installation fees.

While Rachel asked about payment plans, Nikki slipped away to the flowerbeds, her own equipment concealed in a canvas tote. She quickly mounted her camera in the bougainvillea, angling it for the best view of the drive. The pink blooms would hide it once she adjusted the stems.

A rattling trailer interrupted her work. The rig lurched to an abrupt stop only twenty feet away. The driver stepped down from the cab, boots hitting the ground with a confident thud. He yanked open the rear door then emerged leading a gray gelding that coughed as he stumbled down the ramp. The horse's head hung low, yellow discharge draining from both nostrils, a prominent swelling under his jaw.

Nikki's eyes widened at the telltale symptoms. Strangles. One infected horse in the barn and they'd all be quarantined within days.

"Whoa." She stepped forward, blocking his path while keeping a cautious distance. "Your horse looks sick. You'll need to check in at the office."

"Yup. Just need to stick him in a stall first." The handler kept his eyes on the barn door, studying the entrance as if already aware which barn he wanted. The fact that he didn't even pretend concern about his horse confirmed her suspicion. This was deliberate.

"He can't go in a stall," she said. "Not without vet clearance."

"Who's going to stop me?" He yanked the lead rope, urging the sick horse forward.

Gunner trotted stiff-legged from beside the flower bed, his growl ominous. Even the listless horse lifted his head in alarm. But it was the handler's reaction that mattered. And his quick step back showed he wasn't prepared to take on a protective Shepherd.

"Bitch," he muttered. His face darkened then he yanked the horse back onto the trailer, still cursing as he slammed the truck door. He drove away, hitting every rut in the road, taking out his frustration on his equine passenger.

Rachel appeared beside Nikki, her eyes wide. "What was that about? The horse looked terrible."

"Yes, a Trojan horse. Literally."

"They're trying to infect the barn, aren't they?" Rachel scrubbed a hand over her forehead. "Strangles would spread through here in days. I'm surprised Wellington would resort to that. Maybe someone else was involved."

"It's likely someone who knows the workings of a race stable," Nikki said, staring at the dust plumes kicked up by the bouncing trailer. "But who doesn't want to cause permanent damage."

The implications hung heavy. Nikki scanned the parking lot, ensuring they were alone. It was time to push for answers, and possibly figure out what was driving Wellington. "If you want me to keep helping," she said, "I need honesty. Are you using anything—medications, supplements, herbs—that could show up in testing?"

Rachel shook her head, holding Nikki's gaze. But she crossed her arms, hands wrapping around her forearms, and there was an odd expression on her face.

"I can't help you if I don't know," Nikki said, firming her voice.

Rachel pulled in a deep breath, dropping her arms to her sides. "No drugs," she said, her voice almost a whisper even thought they were fifty feet from the barn. But I did use a psychic."

"A psychic?"

"I know how it sounds." Her words tumbled out, as if the admission was painful. "But Conan was so angry in Wellington's barn. The psychic said he felt disrespected, treated like he was low horse in the herd. She told us exactly what he wanted—two salt blocks, double hay nets, straw instead of shavings. He even hated his farrier. Didn't like the way he hammered nails."

"A psychic," Nikki repeated. Her growing tension was replaced by a flood of relief that nearly made her laugh. The double salt blocks and matching hay nets suddenly made sense.

"It's crazy, I know," Rachel said, misunderstanding her reaction. "But apparently Conan saw how Wellington's stakes horses were pampered. And he wanted the same treatment."

"So you did everything the psychic suggested?" Nikki asked, smiling.

"Every single thing. And it worked. He just needs to be treated like he's special. Which he is." Rachel gave a weak laugh. "But can you imagine what Wellington would say if he knew? Using a psychic? I'd be laughed out of racing."

Nikki thought of Sonja's comments, her careful neutrality. The pieces clicked into place. "Your psychic—did you meet her at the track? Is her name Sonja?"

"Yes. Do you know her?"

"I sure do. She's a friend who helped me understand Gunner."

"Please don't tell anyone." Rachel reached out, gripping Nikki's arm. "Sonja promised confidentiality. The racing world would never understand."

"Your secret's safe," Nikki said, unable to stop her smile. At least this wasn't about drugs or corruption. "And this is good news. I've been worried about drug tests. Anything else I should know?"

"No, that's it. Conan's clean." Rachel's chin lifted with pride. "He just has a trainer crazy enough to listen to a psychic. Though his demands were very specific. Who knew a horse cared about matching salt blocks?"

Nikki kept smiling long after Rachel returned to the barn. The revelation about psychic consultations cleared up so much, not only Conan's peculiar stall arrangements but also Sonja's evasiveness. She knelt in front of the flower bed, fingers working efficiently to conceal her camera among the blooms, still amused at the thought of a racehorse demanding interior design specifics.

Then her phone buzzed and Justin's text hit like a gut punch: *Checked out Rachel. No drug violations but her ex-husband is paralyzed. Conan put him in a wheelchair last October.*

Nikki stared at the screen, struggling to absorb the words, her relief about psychic consultations fizzling. This was bigger than training methods or a horse's quirks. Conan had left a man permanently disabled. Wellington's campaign suddenly carried new weight. Maybe he wasn't protecting his reputation. Maybe he really was trying to prevent another tragedy.

And she didn't have the patience to cut through any more of Rachel's deflections. It was time to talk to Wellington, figure out his motivations. Before someone else was hurt.

CHAPTER SIX

Nikki pulled into the owners' parking lot and snagged a prime spot close to the backside. Santa Anita training hours ran from five to ten am, and the oval was nearly deserted except for two tractors methodically grooming the surface. Wellington usually exercised his top horses just after five when the track was freshly harrowed, though he'd adjust his schedule if an owner insisted on watching at a later time, or if he was looking for media attention. With any luck, she'd catch him at his barn.

She leashed Gunner and headed to the backside, still gathering her thoughts. She'd been mulling about Rachel's ex-husband the entire drive back from Mountain View. A paralyzed man changed everything. If Conan was truly dangerous, Wellington's campaign against him made sense. And his determination to keep the horse from racing wasn't based on jealousy.

The morning had warmed and most of the barns were quiet. A few horses still circled on mechanical hot walkers, the hollow thuds of their hooves blending with mariachi music drifting from the grooms' dorms. Perfect time for a conversation about a horse that might be more dangerous than Rachel cared to admit.

Wellington's shedrow was perfectly raked, with a herringbone design decorating the dirt. Color-coordinated coolers and bright bandages hung from clotheslines. Sleek horses contentedly tugged at their hay nets, more interested in their lunch than a human visitor. There was no sign of Wellington's distinctive silver hair.

"Looking for the boss?" a vaguely familiar groom asked, his voice polite but guarded. Clearly word had spread about Nikki's involvement with Rachel. "He headed over to the kitchen about twenty minutes ago."

Nikki thanked him, feeling his eyes following her progress until she was well away from the barn. The groom wasn't just an employee. He was a longtime Wellington loyalist, rightly protective of his employer and horses, giving the kind of allegiance money can't buy.

The smell of frying bacon grew stronger as she approached the kitchen. She veered through the parking lot and around to the back where several gnarled oak trees provided patches of shade. She was just about to leave Gunner in a stay command when the rear door swung open and a familiar woman stepped out.

"My two favorite visitors," Andrea Lopez called, wiping her hands on her apron. "It's busy now. Want me to grab you a coffee? Skip the lineup?"

"No need," Nikki said. Ever since she and Gunner had rescued Andrea's son, the woman couldn't do enough for her. "I'm looking for James Wellington. Is he inside?"

Andrea nodded, a smile curving her pretty face. "The Wellingtons just made another big donation to the rec hall and they're offering scholarships to our kids. Ricky's going to apply."

"That's wonderful. Let us know if he needs a personal reference." Nikki gave a thumbs-up and signaled for Gunner to stay. It was convenient Andrea was on break. Gunner wouldn't be alone for long, and he was comfortable with her.

The screen door squeaked as Nikki entered the kitchen. Steam rose from industrial coffee makers while short-order cooks shouted rapid orders. Conversations in Spanish and English competed with a hissing grill and the clatter of plates.

She spotted Wellington immediately, his Barbour jacket and crisp khakis setting him apart from the work-worn crowd of grooms and hotwalkers. Heads turned and conversations dropped as she crossed the room. No one even pretended not to be interested.

Wellington's gaze flicked up, cool and assessing. "Hello, Nikki. I assume this isn't a social call."

"No. I'd like to talk about Conan."

His fingers tightened on his coffee cup. Then he pushed it aside. "Not in here."

He rose and led her outside to a secluded corner of the parking lot, where dumpsters blocked all view from the kitchen. The breeze carried a mix of hay and rotting food, surrounded by buzzing flies. Not much chance of being disturbed here, Nikki thought.

"I know about your involvement with Rachel Parker," Wellington said, an accusing edge cutting his voice. "Did you know Conan grabbed my groom? Not just a nip. He took flesh. And that wasn't as bad as the gate crew member he trampled."

He stepped closer, his cologne failing to mask the scent of his anger. "And Mountain View's owner? Rachel Parker's ex?" he went on. "Do you know what the horse did to him?"

Nikki held her ground, irritated at his entitled aggression. Wellington spoke as if he owned the track, as if his family name granted him authority.

"I heard he was paralyzed," she said, her voice measured.

"Yet she still makes her teenage daughter ride," Wellington said. "That woman has no experience with problem horses, no proper help. And now she's aiming for the Derby."

He slammed a fist into his palm, scattering the buzzing flies. "My Saudi clients are threatening to move their horses to Kentucky. They won't risk their three-year-olds in a starting gate with that brute. Conan's a powder keg. I've trained his type. They behave just long enough to lower your guard then someone else ends up crippled. Or dead."

His eyes locked on hers. "I trained that horse for five months—I know he's too dangerous to set foot on a track. And I'm not stopping until she retires him. If you really care about racing, you might want to reconsider whose side you're on."

He stomped back to the kitchen, his leather boots kicking up dust. Nikki rubbed her forehead, her mind racing. A paralyzed ex-husband who she'd just learned owned Mountain View. Nervous Saudi owners threatening to leave. And a trainer whose composure cracked at the mention of a horse's name.

Somewhere in all the accusations lay the truth about Conan. And she needed to find it. Because Wellington's warning might not be about protecting his reputation, or his wealthy clients. He seemed to truly believe someone else would get hurt.

CHAPTER SEVEN

Cricket song filled the evening air as Nikki carried a bowl of salad through the sliding glass doors to their small patio. The herbs she'd planted last spring scented the breeze: basil, oregano, rosemary climbing out of their pots. The scent of grilling meat mixed with the sweet fragrance of night-blooming jasmine. A neighbor's wind chimes tinkled, carrying on the evening breeze.

It was a soothing contrast to the track kitchen and Wellington's bubbling anger. Here in their backyard sanctuary, those tensions felt distant.

Justin stood at the grill, beer in hand, watching steaks sizzle. These moments were always precious after the intensity of their work days, a reminder that normal life existed outside of threats and investigations.

Gunner patrolled the fenced yard's perimeter, snuffling at the ground as he checked his territory. Every few moments he'd pause, head lifting toward the street, always on duty.

Nikki understood how he felt. She couldn't shake Wellington's expression, the way his control had shattered when talking about Conan. That kind of visceral reaction often led to disproportionate responses—people convinced of danger sometimes created it, their fear driving them to extremes far beyond what was warranted. If Wellington truly believed Conan posed a threat, to what lengths might he go?

Justin also looked preoccupied, his shoulders tight beneath his LAPD t-shirt. His face maintained its strong-featured handsomeness, the angular jaw line and intelligent eyes that caught a lot of women's attention. Only his body betrayed the strain—tension revealed through an unusual stiffness as he tended the grill.

He preferred to leave it at the precinct and rarely brought the darkness home so his current homicide case must be hitting hard. But he liked to hear about her work, offering insights without trying to direct her actions. One of the many things she loved about him was his ability to be both detective and partner without letting one overpower the other.

"Rough day?" she asked, setting the salad on the table. The fresh mozzarella and tomatoes gleamed with olive oil and balsamic, another attempt at normal routine.

"Better now." His intimate smile made her heart skip. "Tell me what Wellington had to say."

Nikki settled into a patio chair, watching Justin expertly flip the steaks. The grill's heat pushed back the gathering coolness and she stretched out her legs, determined to relax. "Wellington seems just as worried about his Saudi clients as he is about Conan's behavior. They're threatening to move their horses east if Conan runs in the Derby."

"Makes sense." Justin handed her a cold beer, the tasty Canadian brew was one of their shared indulgences. "No owner wants their horses in a starting gate with a dangerous one. Too much at risk."

"But Conan seems perfectly behaved now. This morning he galloped like a veteran, completely focused on his job."

"Horses react differently to stress." Justin moved the steaks to a cooler spot on the grill, adjusting the heat with the competence he brought to everything. "Did Wellington mention Conan's breeding?"

"No, why?"

"Because his sire stands in Kentucky. Owned by Wellington's client and commands huge stud fees. The sire was known to be hot-headed but if breeders start thinking his offspring are unstable..." He let the implications hang.

Nikki sat straighter. "The stud fee would plummet."

"And Wellington's client would lose millions, not only in stud fees but at auction," Justin said. "No one wants to buy a yearling that might turn dangerous. Or breed to a stallion whose offspring could hurt someone."

Gunner's bark interrupted her response. He stood rigid, staring at the jasmine that climbed their back fence. Probably another cat, but after today's revelations, every shadow felt threatening. Before she could check what had caught his attention, her phone buzzed—an alert from her surveillance camera at Mountain View.

She clicked the notification, watching as a van stopped in front of the barn—a vehicle that had come from the direction of the house. Through the grainy night vision, she saw the side door slide open and a lift extend.

A man in a wheelchair rolled forward, his arm movements jerky. Light spilled from Conan's barn as Marco stepped out to meet him.

"From the camera at Mountain View," she murmured, angling the phone so Justin could see.

"Must be Rachel's ex," Justin said, moving behind her chair to watch the screen. "First time he's shown up?"

"That I know of. But Rachel didn't tell me he owned the facility. Didn't mention him at all."

Nikki increased the volume, but the audio only caught fragments of raised voices. The wheelchair-bound man pointed repeatedly toward the barn, his gestures authoritative.

"I see the plate," Justin said "Want me run it?"

"Can you hear what he's saying?"

"Not clearly. But it's obvious he's upset." Justin touched her shoulder. "Forward me the feed. I'll run his name. See what the police report says about his accident."

"Accident?" The word felt wrong. "You mean when Conan hurt him?"

"Maybe." Justin's tone was careful, measured. "But if a horse puts someone in a wheelchair, there's usually a lawsuit."

On screen, Marco stood his ground in the doorway, his body language protective rather than confrontational. The man in the wheelchair stopped rolling forward when his wheels stalled in the dirt, but his frustrated gesture needed no audio to interpret.

"Apparently he owns Mountain View," Nikki said. "That explains why Rachel has trained out of there so long. Wonder what's bothering him."

"Marco's handling it well," Justin said, his gaze still fixed on the screen. "Staying calm, keeping himself between the barn and—" He broke off as Rachel appeared in the frame. She walked toward her ex-husband, her stride purposeful.

The man in the wheelchair said something and waved his arm, the motion almost pleading. Rachel shook her head and walked away. He watched her go then rolled back to the van, defeat evident in the slump of his shoulders.

"That was interesting," Nikki said as the van circled and disappeared from sight. "It doesn't look like Rachel is afraid of him but there was something else there."

"History between them runs deep." Justin returned to the grill and began plating their dinner. The steaks had rested perfectly, juice pooling on the warmed plates.

"She didn't seem surprised by the visit," Nikki said, still watching the surveillance feed.

"Could be he misses her." Justin's tone was thoughtful as he set their supper on the table. "The way he reached toward her before leaving. That wasn't anger. That was longing."

"But Rachel keeps her distance. Doesn't appear to want much to do with him. And it's odd she didn't mention he owned Mountain View. I heard that from Wellington."

"Family dynamics can be complicated," Justin said. "Especially when horses are involved. And Mountain View isn't just a training facility. It's where their marriage fell apart."

Nikki watched the screen, now showing only an empty road. Tomorrow she'd drive back to the center and get some answers. And a talk with Kat might be helpful. But tonight, the mystery would have to wait.

"Let's not let these steaks get cold," she said, setting down her phone. "Or Gunner will be one happy dog." At his name, Gunner's tail thumped hopefully against the deck, his nose twitching at the scent of grilled meat.

They ate in companionable silence. But Nikki's thoughts kept returning to the surveillance footage. "Marco didn't seem too worried."

Justin nodded. "The ex-husband showing up at night, Marco ready at the door—it's likely not the first time. Regular enough that they have a routine for handling it. Obviously still some strong emotion."

Her phone buzzed again. Another alert from Mountain View, but this time it was only Rachel slipping into her car and heading home. The barn sat peacefully in the camera's night vision, Conan safe in his stall, watched by Marco. But too many secrets surrounded that horse for Nikki to believe the calm would last.

"I'm going to look into the center's ownership records and accident reports," she said. "Maybe Rachel and her ex are still tied together and have to communicate. And maybe he's worried about Conan hurting someone again."

"Sometimes," Justin said, "what looks like the obvious distracts us from what's really going on. Like your surveillance setup catching the visit. Important, but maybe not for the reasons we think."

Nikki studied Justin's face. With his impressive solve rate and years working homicide, he'd developed an instinct for when surface facts concealed deeper truths. "You think there's more to his visits than checking on the barn?"

"I think a man doesn't show up at night just to argue about property management." He took a swig of beer. "And a woman doesn't stand there absorbing his words unless some part of her needs to hear them."

Nikki thought about Rachel's avoidance issue, Kat's guarded ways and now Jim's night visit that seemed more about connection than confrontation.

"Rachel never did tell me about that accident with Conan," she said. "You dug it up and then Wellington mentioned it. I guess she's so used to information being used against her that she's learned to hold back. Kat too."

Shaking her head, she reached across the table for Justin's hand, knowing they both needed to disconnect from their work and enjoy this reprieve. His fingers linked with hers, the gentle stroke of his thumb against her palm saying everything words couldn't.

The night settled around them, stars emerging one by one. For these moments, she could pretend the issues at Mountain View weren't growing larger with each hour. But she knew better. And the peace they enjoyed tonight felt as fragile as the jasmine blossoms that would wilt by morning.

CHAPTER EIGHT

Morning traffic crawled along the freeway, brake lights stretching endlessly as Nikki inched her car toward Mountain View. Last night's surveillance footage left her with more questions than answers. While stuck in this turtle-paced commute, a call to Sonja might shed some light.

She pressed the hands-free button. Sonja answered on the first ring.

"I was expecting your call," Sonja said, her voice lifting with amusement. "Knew it wouldn't take you long to dig up my involvement with Rachel. But you know I can't discuss clients."

"I'm not asking about Rachel," Nikki said. "I'm worried about Conan hurting someone. Kat, his jockey—"

Sonja's laugh cut her off. "Is that what's bothering you? Trust me, Conan's not dangerous. He actually prefers female riders, responds better to a light touch."

"But Wellington insists he's dangerous."

"Wellington never understood him," Sonja said, her tone suggesting deeper knowledge. "Conan's like a teenager. Sulks when ignored, shines when respected. Rachel gives him the star treatment he craves."

No doubt that was true. In Wellington's barn, Conan had been one of many. As an unproven two-year-old he would have been low on the totem pole. Rachel only had one horse so Conan received all the attention. And Wellington's ego would make it difficult to accept that another trainer could achieve such a turnaround.

Nikki blew out a calming breath. Sonja's insights weren't always conventional but she'd learned to trust them. But there was still one other issue. "What about the paralyzed ex-husband?"

"Not my story to tell." Sonja's tone turned serious. "But don't let Wellington's version cloud your judgment. There are probably four sides to that story."

"Thanks, Sonja." Their conversation drifted to other topics: The old donkey Sonja had rescued who was finally eating again, her brother's progress in rehab, and the possibility of a big payout in the sixth race today. By the time they ended the call, traffic had thinned and Nikki had left behind the billboards and strip malls and office towers.

She was still turning over questions about the wheelchair accident, and more importantly, Conan's role in it, when she pulled into Mountain View's parking lot. A westerly wind carried the rhythmic sound of horses moving in their stalls, punctuated by an occasional nickered greeting.

Kat jogged from the barn, school bag swinging. She skidded to a stop when she spotted them.

"You missed the gate training session!" Her voice bubbled with pride as she dropped to one knee and patted Gunner. "Conan was so good. Mom uses this systematic program. First just walking him past the gate then standing quietly inside. Today we had flags waving, cans full of rocks rattling, even speakers playing recorded crowd noise. He just stood there, totally calm."

Nikki's estimation of Rachel rose further. Some trainers pushed horses through gates, hoping repetition would cure fear. But Rachel followed a thoughtful desensitization program, building layers of confidence through careful exposure—the type of individual approach that could transform a truly challenging horse. It showed a level of horsemanship far beyond what she'd expected from a small-time trainer.

"Your mom thinks of everything," Nikki said. "And this seems like a great facility for specialized training where you can work at each horse's pace. I understand your father owns the center?"

Kat rose, her smile gone. "Jim is not my father! Just Mom's ex-husband." She crossed her arms, rigid with the defensive posture she was so quick to display. The carefree teenager had vanished, replaced by a young woman shouldering adult burdens. "Now he thinks Conan's success means he deserves half ownership."

"I understand he's in a wheelchair because of the horse."

"That wasn't Conan's fault." Kat's voice held a brittle edge. She backed toward her car, her gaze darting toward the office. "I have to go. Mom won't let me keep riding Conan if I'm late for school."

Her mood shift seemed about more than just disliking a stepfather. She'd gone from enthusiastic to guarded the moment Jim was mentioned. Clearly Wellington was wrong about one thing though. No one was forcing Kat to ride Conan. That was just a mean-spirited rumor.

Nikki turned toward the office building next to the grandstand. Jim Turner, Rachel's ex, would be a key ally in securing the facility, and she needed to establish a working relationship. She was equally interested in meeting the man himself. Kat's reaction to his name signaled a deep rift. Understanding the tension between Mountain View's owner and Rachel's daughter might prove as important as any security protocol.

The office was an older building that had been recently retrofitted with a widened doorway and ramp. It had a commanding view of the track as well as the mountain trails that wound into the foothills, a view that must taunt someone newly confined to a chair.

The solid door bore a prominent sign: Office Hours: 6 am to 12 Noon. It was barely past nine and the parking lot was empty except for Jim's specialized van, the same vehicle she'd seen on last night's surveillance video.

She pressed the automatic door opener, located below a key panel. The door swung wide and she was greeted by the faint trace of perfume. An office divider separated the reception area from a private workspace. The layout was wheelchair friendly, everything with easy access, including an elaborate coffee machine. A sturdy desk was positioned to greet visitors and dominated the reception area.

Framed photographs lined the walls with Jim astride various horses before his accident, receiving trophies at local shows and standing arm-in-arm with Rachel at what appeared to be a track fundraiser. Most striking was a large panoramic shot of Mountain View at sunrise, the San Gabriel Mountains rising majestically behind the property, capturing both its current beauty and its potential.

A young woman glanced up from the computer, her nightclub attire and perfect manicure jarring against the rural setting. The desk nametag said Sophia Mendez. "May I help you?" she asked, her welcoming smile not quite reaching her eyes.

"I have some questions about your facility." Nikki said, noting how the woman's eyes flicked toward the divider.

"We're full." Bangles jangled as she gestured to a clipboard. "I can add you to the waitlist. But it could be up to a year. And active racing Thoroughbreds take preference."

"Actually, I'm hoping to speak to Jim Turner about security."

"That's me." Jim wheeled around the divider. She recognized him immediately from the surveillance footage—the same broad shoulders and chiseled features now arranged in a charming smile not visible in last night's grainy video. In person, he projected an easy confidence that the camera hadn't captured. But his smile slipped when he saw Gunner.

"So you're the PI with the dog. The one Rachel can't stop talking about, here to save the day." His eyes glittered with surprising hostility. "Maybe you can convince her to sell that brute before someone else gets hurt."

"I understand Conan injured you," Nikki said carefully.

"His first month here." Bitterness hardened his voice. "Rachel's daughter shouldn't have been riding him. He was uncontrollable."

"I'm sorry," she said. The words felt hollow against such devastating change. Before her sat a man who'd previously lived for the physical: riding, training, managing the track. Now he was forced to watch from the sidelines while Rachel moved forward without him, finding success with the very horse that had destroyed his world.

"Don't want to talk about it." Jim's knuckles whitened over the arms of his chair. "Don't want anything to do with that animal. And as far as security goes, we have smoke detectors, sprinklers and an excellent night watchman. Since Rachel prefers outside help these days, maybe she should hire her own guard. I sure as hell can't walk around and do it."

The young woman, Sophia, moved protectively toward him. The gesture was intimate, possessive. Clearly they were more than employee and boss.

"You can show her out." Jim spun his wheelchair in dismissal and rolled behind the divider. Sophia's frosty stare left no room for further questions.

Nikki stepped back into the sunshine, sucking in a breath of fresh air as she mulled over his words. Jim's bitterness seemed focused on Conan, not Rachel. In fact his voice had softened at the mention of her name. But he'd referred to Kat as "Rachel's daughter," distancing himself from the teen.

She trudged back toward Conan's barn, relaxing with every step that carried her further from the office. A ginger cat dozed on a weathered chair, undisturbed by her passing. An exercise rider lounged on top of a picnic table, paperback on her chest, water bottle dangling loosely in her fingers. In a nearby paddock, a chestnut horse rolled with pleasure, legs flailing skyward.

Away from the office's charged atmosphere, she could appreciate a freedom rarely found at the track. Grass to graze, space to relax, mountain trails to explore. Though she would only trust an experienced trail horse on those steep paths. Racehorses were trained for explosive speed, and surprises could trigger flight instincts.

The quiet purr of a car yanked her back. A black Mercedes cruised into the small parking lot in front of Conan's barn, its tinted windows resembling dark mirrors. The car settled into a spot next to Rachel's truck, engine idling for a moment before falling silent.

Two men emerged, their suits tailored but clearly chosen for function over fashion. The taller one adjusted his jacket, the movement drawing Nikki's attention to the telltale bulge of a shoulder holster. These weren't casual visitors admiring horses, or lost hikers searching for the trailhead.

"We are looking for Rachel Parker." The shorter man addressed Nikki, his English formal and precise. "We represent Sheikh Abdullah."

"That's me," Rachel stepped from the barn, curiosity evident in the tilt of her head.

"Ms. Parker?" The shorter man inclined his head with careful respect. "We would like to purchase your three-year-old colt. The one called Conan."

"He isn't for sale." Rachel's voice carried polite firmness, along with the tone of someone who was used to making decisions. And sticking to them.

"Perhaps we could discuss this privately." The man gestured toward the Mercedes, more as a command than an invitation. "Our offer will be substantial."

Rachel's chin lifted. "Money isn't the issue. But please thank the Sheikh for his interest." She started to turn away, but the taller man stepped forward, his movement bringing the shoulder holster into sharper relief.

"The Sheikh is concerned about your horse competing in the Santa Anita Derby." His voice held an edge his companion's had lacked. "He feels retirement would be best for all involved."

"He's not retiring." Rachel's arms crossed, her stance matching her resolute tone. "And he isn't for sale."

The men exchanged measured looks that spoke volumes. "We will relay your response. Though the Sheikh may be disappointed."

They returned to the Mercedes, their polished shoes incongruous against the packed dirt. As they drove away, the car's windows reflected nothing but darkness, as opaque as the power behind their polite threat.

Nikki watched them disappear, filled with the familiar dread she felt when violence lurked beneath fake civility. She checked on Rachel, who stood straight backed in the doorway, showing no sign of intimidation. Unlike her nervous reaction to the vehicles yesterday, she now projected complete confidence in Nikki's protection.

But that trust left Nikki's stomach churning. Three different threats to Conan had emerged in just twenty-four hours: Wellington with his racing connections, Jim with his bitter grudge, and now armed emissaries from Saudi Arabia.

The real question wasn't which one would strike first. It was whether she could identify the danger in time.

CHAPTER NINE

Rachel gave a slow head shake as she stared at the receding Mercedes. "I can't believe this is happening. Last month no one cared about Conan."

She ran a hand through her hair, her confidence from moments ago wavering. "I never wanted all this attention. The reporters, the phone calls, people watching our every move. I just wanted to train my horse. Even if this mess with Wellington resolves itself, I don't think I'll ever get used to recorders in my face and cameras tracking every step. Some trainers thrive on that spotlight, but I'm just not built for it."

"Wellington's smear campaign backfired," Nikki said, following her into the barn. "He made Conan sound so dangerous that now everyone's paying attention."

"That's just it." Rachel stopped in front of Conan's stall, her fingers trailing over the lead line hanging on his door. "Now everyone thinks he's some kind of monster. But look at him." She gestured to where the colt dozed in the corner, one hind leg tilted at rest. "Does he look dangerous to you?"

"He put your ex-husband in a wheelchair," Nikki said, keeping a prudent distance from the stall. The big colt looked peaceful enough, but she'd been around enough stallions to know their unpredictability—standing quietly one moment then lunging with bared teeth the next. A lifetime around horses had taught her to respect their size and strength. She couldn't afford to let Rachel's faith cloud her judgment. Not with armed men making threats and three different adversaries circling.

"Kat swears that wasn't Conan's fault. I saw them heading toward the track that day. He was relaxed, walking on a loose rein. Marco and I had cut through the barns toward the bleachers so we could watch his gallop. We heard shouting but by the time we got there, Jim was on the ground. It was awful."

"But you still let Kat ride him? Weren't you afraid he'd hurt her?"

"Not one bit. Conan was different from the moment he arrived here. Like a switch had been flipped. He loves having three people fussing over him, treating him like he's the only horse in our stable." A rueful smile touched her face. "Which he is. The psychic helped us understand that he wasn't vicious. He'd just been rebelling. Like an overactive kid who needs tons of attention. She said Conan is actually quite protective of Kat. Views her as part of his herd."

"Kat made it clear she doesn't think much of Jim," Nikki said, watching Rachel's expression. "Was she reluctant to come back here when you bought Conan?"

Rachel's face tightened, that familiar guardedness flickering across her features. She hesitated, fingers twisting the lead rope as she weighed her response. Then something softened in her eyes, the beginning of trust.

"Yes," Rachel said. "But she was fine once she saw how well Conan responded. And she knows money is tight." She took a deep breath, offering more than she had before. "After the divorce, Kat kept everything inside. Wouldn't talk about Jim. I still don't know exactly what happened that day. She insists Conan spooked, but she gets defensive when I ask for details. And Jim's memory is still a blur."

She turned back to Conan, who shuffled to the front of the stall, blinking sleepily but hopeful for a treat. No sign of the dangerous outlaw in Wellington's stories. "Jim would love it if I sold," Rachel said. "Thinks he deserves compensation for the accident. And I'd like to give him something. But Kat would never forgive me if I sold this horse."

"You couldn't find a stall at another training center?"

"This place has a good track and the price is right. The divorce settlement guarantees me access. Luckily Wellington has no influence here. Jim never cared much about the actual racing. Before the accident, his way of relaxing was a trail ride in the mountains. That's where I fell in love with him."

Nikki hesitated, weighing the need for information against professional boundaries. But personal questions often unlocked key details. And Rachel was finally opening up. "Why did you divorce?"

Rachel dropped the lead, its metal snap bouncing against the door. "Found a thong in our bed. It wasn't mine." Her face closed off. "Thought I knew him. Thought he'd be a good father figure. But I've moved on. Now I just want to focus on Kat and horses."

Nikki watched her coil the lead, the kind of mindless movement that helped soothe memories. Every mention of Jim seemed to carry layers of meaning: a combination of regret, anger and guilt. Jim's bitterness toward Conan might be less about his injury and more about losing his wife. And maybe he was jealous of Rachel's success, especially since he could no longer ride a horse.

"I gather you don't have to push Kat to ride Conan?" Nikki said, easing toward a more comfortable topic.

Rachel grinned, her smile genuine this time. "Of course not. But she knows if her school grades drop, she'll have to stop. I'm not even going to tell her about the Sheikh's offer. She'd be too worried." The smile slid from her face. "On the other hand, Jim would be better off if I sold Conan. The divorce was final four months before the accident but I'd gift him money because of what happened. Right now though, that's not an option. I'm broke and he knows it."

Conan stretched his muscled neck over the stall door and nudged Rachel's shoulder, still hoping for a mint. He didn't look like he was poised to grab a hunk of flesh. In fact, he was exceptionally polite for a young stallion.

Rachel scratched the bottom of his jaw, and he lowered his head even further, demonstrating mutual trust. The gossip around this woman seemed even more vindictive, especially the part where Wellington said she'd forced her daughter to ride a dangerous horse.

"Guess I need to worry about more than just Wellington's campaign," Rachel said. "Those men today weren't making idle threats. And Jim is turning aggressive about pushing a sale. Says if Conan hurts anyone here, he'll be liable."

"You think Jim would want to hurt Conan?"

"No! He loves horses. But he's trying to change my mind about selling. He actually came by here last night. Drove over in a special van that a public fundraiser made possible. Turned a little emotional."

Nikki nodded. She knew about Jim's visit, but Rachel's new openness was welcome. It was much easier to protect clients when they didn't hold back. "Were you worried?"

"No. He's just frustrated. He used to always be around the barns, eager to ride with anyone who wanted to get out on the trails. Now he's stuck in the office, staring out a window. But once the insurance company approves his claim, he'll be able to afford more things. Get back into some old routines."

"Is his insurance through the center's policy?"

"Yes. But they limited future coverage since Conan knocked him down."

Nikki absently patted Gunner's head, trying to picture the scene. She'd watched Kat and Conan working together, their fluid partnership, the way the horse responded to his rider's lightest cue. Something didn't add up. "So it wasn't a strike or kick? I'm surprised Kat lost control."

Rachel sighed. "Her reins were too long. She wasn't expecting him to bolt. And she feels so guilty. Hasn't been the same since."

She gestured toward the rear of the barn. "That horse path leads to the track but it also circles the property. Nearly sixty acres of flat groomed footing. It's a big reason why so many people want stalls here."

She shook her head, her voice thick with regret. "Before the accident, Kat and her friends would stay out for hours, chatting and laughing while they cooled out their horses. Now it's all business. She goes straight from home to barn to school. Like she's afraid to enjoy horses again. But I really don't think she's scared of Conan."

"I hear there was another incident. Wellington said Conan trampled someone around the starting gate?"

"Yes, an assistant starter, Tommy Garcia. But Tommy told me it wasn't such a big deal. It was during a gate approval session and they were rushing. Conan also got worked up in his first race with Wellington. Had a false start but I watched the video. He was scared, not mean. We've done so much ground work since. If you have time, drop by tomorrow and watch his gallop."

"I will," Nikki said. She'd have to leave the city much earlier than she had this morning but at least she'd beat the traffic. "Is Marco all set for another night? Are you good with the security we discussed?"

"Everything's working fine." Rachel glanced at the new camera mounted close to Conan's stall. "I keep the feed locked in my car and Marco's grabbing some sleep now. I've got his coffee thermos filled for tonight. We're keeping a good watch. Doing everything you said."

Nikki nodded but made a sweep of the area around the barn, checking each access point and even testing paddock latches. The Saudi visit had rattled her more than she wanted to admit. And after her tense conversation with Jim, it was clear they couldn't count on security help from the owner. But Rachel was sitting outside Conan's stall, his feed was locked up and cameras covered the area.

She gave Rachel a final wave before she and Gunner headed back to the city. But as the training center faded in her rearview mirror, the knot in her stomach returned. Rachel's explanation about Jim seemed reasonable, but those two trampling incidents kept flashing through her mind. Images formed unbidden—a child at the rail, Marco in the paddock, an accident during the post parade with thousands watching. If Conan hurt someone in the Derby after she'd helped get him there...

Her fingers drummed against the steering wheel, the rhythm matching her churning thoughts. Wellington's warnings about Conan no longer seemed like mere jealousy or wounded pride—not after seeing Jim confined to that wheelchair. The possibility that Conan posed a danger couldn't be dismissed as easily as she'd hoped.

Jim's accident might have been complicated by circumstances—a brash young horse adjusting to new surroundings, perhaps mishandled. But the gate incident should be straightforward, documented, witnessed by professionals. If Conan had deliberately attacked a crew member, it would be impossible for her to ignore.

She turned her car toward Santa Anita, sifting through her options. The track would be quiet now but she should be able to find someone who could point her to Tommy Garcia. Gate crew members knew every horse that came through their hands, and they talked among themselves about the difficult ones.

If Tommy had witnessed a genuinely dangerous horse, he would have shared that information with his colleagues. And unlike Rachel or Wellington, he had no personal stake in Conan's reputation. She needed the unvarnished truth from someone who'd been on the receiving end of Conan's supposed aggression. And someone who had nothing to gain by lying.

When she arrived at Santa Anita, she parked in the owners' lot and walked to the far end of the grandstand. Training hours were over and the oval was empty except for two tractors grooming the surface. The starting gate sat positioned just before the eighth pole, where several men huddled around it, checking one of the wheels. The massive metal structure always looked ominous to Nikki—fourteen steel stalls designed to contain 1200-pound animals in moments of peak anxiety. No wonder things sometimes went wrong.

"Can you help?" she called. "I'm looking for Tommy Garcia."

A wiry man in a track jacket with a radio clipped on his belt grinned and jerked his thumb toward Clockers' Corner. "Try the coffee crowd."

The breakfast tables by the rail were still busy despite the late hour, filled with racing's lifers sharing theories and coffee beneath striped umbrellas. Track regulars gathered at Clockers' Corner every morning, joined by interested fans who knew this was the best spot to glimpse the racing world. Voices rose and fell as they dissected workout times and the newest training methods.

She recognized a couple of the gate crew among the group, all of them with radios. One of them waved her over.

"I'm Tommy. Heard you're looking for me." He had Latin features, curious eyes and the lean build of a lifetime horseman. "What can I do for you?"

"I'm looking into an incident with Conan. Happened last fall, during gate approvals. I understand there was some trouble."

"Oh yeah, the big bay." Tommy settled back in his chair. "I had a hold of his tail, trying to push him in when things went wrong. He came out the back, fast and hard. My fault really, should've waited for more help with a horse that size." He shrugged. "Wellington made a big deal about it, but the colt just knocked me down. Bruised my hip pretty good and they put me in concussion protocol. Thank God for helmet and flak jacket rules."

"So he didn't deliberately trample you?"

"Nah, he actually stopped and looked around, like he was surprised to see me on the ground." Tommy reached for his coffee. "Look, that horse has a reputation so Wellington assumed the worst. But those gates are scary to horses, especially two-year-olds. They're a flight or fight animal. If they can't run away, the best ones will fight. It's that kind of spirit that makes a winner. No worries, we don't ban horses for incidents like that. The new trainer already talked to me, making sure the horse wasn't on our list."

The knot in Nikki's stomach loosened. Tommy's frank assessment matched Rachel's version. A gate incident with a young, high-strung horse was hardly proof of vicious tendencies.

But it didn't explain the deeper currents she'd observed at Mountain View. And that October morning still held gaps: Rachel and Marco heading to the bleachers, Kat alone on Conan's back, Jim tragically ending up beneath powerful hooves.

Clearly there were pieces of a darker puzzle still missing. And her mind wouldn't rest until they were uncovered.

CHAPTER TEN

Nikki's office felt like a tomb after the morning's intensity at Mountain View and the buzz of Santa Anita's Clockers' Corner. She sat at her desk, half-eaten sandwich forgotten as she stared at her monitor lit by the glow of multiple browser tabs—local news archives, insurance records and property documents. Somewhere in these digital files lay information about Jim Turner's accident.

Her conversation with Tommy Garcia had settled some concerns about Conan's gate behavior, but it had only deepened the mystery surrounding the wheelchair incident. The assistant starter's casual dismissal of the idea the horse tried to harm him contrasted with Jim's opinion of Conan.

The local news archive yielded sparse results for 'Mountain View Training Center accident October' and other search variations. A few brief mentions in the racing section caught her eye, mostly rehashing the same vague details. One police blotter entry noted emergency response to the facility.

Finally, buried in the fourth page of search results, a longer article emerged. *Local Horseman Injured in Training Accident*. The piece included quotes from Ashley Robart, a seventeen-year-old exercise rider who'd witnessed the incident: "I was just getting back from cooling out my horse," Ashley had told the reporter. "Kat's horse spooked and bolted. Like they said, it happened so fast. One minute everything was normal, the next minute Mr. Turner was on the ground."

Something about the media account felt off. The girl had collaborated both Jim and Kat's version of events, but the statement felt too neat. And it seemed odd that no one had mentioned this witness before. Then again, Nikki hadn't specifically asked about witnesses. Rachel and Jim probably assumed she was investigating security issues and Wellington's claims, not questioning the accident itself.

Nikki kept digging, clicking through links until she found a GoFundMe page that Rachel had created: *Help a respected horseman rebuild his life.* The profile opened with a striking photo of Jim in healthier days—tanned and handsome astride a buckskin horse, mountains rising behind him as he flashed his camera-ready smile. The contrast with the hospital photo below was jarring: Jim pale against white sheets, medical equipment crowding the room, his athletic frame looking small and vulnerable.

A list of required modifications followed: ramps, lifts, bathroom renovations, vehicle conversion. The estimated costs made her eyes widen, but the donors' comments showed how respected Jim was in the local horse community. The before and after images painted a compelling story of tragedy, one that had clearly touched many hearts.

Nikki leaned back in her chair, staring through the window at the lone afternoon cloud drifting across the sky. Rachel clearly felt both guilt and responsibility, evident in her fundraising appeal. Despite their divorce, she'd taken responsibility for helping Jim rebuild his life. And people had responded generously. The specialized van alone would have cost a small fortune.

Nikki pulled out her phone and called Rachel, wanting information about the young witness who might hold critical clues about Jim's accident.

"Ashley Parker?" Rachel's voice was matter-of-fact when she answered, no evidence of tension. "She was a great friend of Kat's but unfortunately she left before Christmas. A lot of kids come and go. Early mornings aren't for everyone."

"Did she ride for different people? Or one trainer in particular?"

"She galloped for anyone who wanted her. Just another horse crazy kid. She was one of the bolder ones who cooled the horses out by riding on the trails. Had a lovely seat, nice hands. Bubbly personality. If Kat hadn't insisted on riding Conan, I would have asked Ashley. I think she and the horse would have gotten along great."

The praise seemed genuine, which made Ashley's abrupt departure seem puzzling.

"May I have Kat's number?"

"Of course." Rachel recited the number, her tone shifting to distraction. "But she's still at school. She usually turns her phone off during class."

"Thanks. I just have a few questions about the accident."

"No problem." The sound of splashing water carried through the phone. Rachel was likely helping Marco scrub Conan's buckets. The groom insisted Conan's water be freshened three times a day.

Nikki cut the connection and tried Kat's number, encouraged when she answered on the first ring. But the teenager's enthusiasm disappeared the moment she heard the reason for Nikki's call.

"Ashley Robart? Why her? Lots of girls rode there."

"She witnessed your stepfather's accident."

Long silence filled the line, heavy with unspoken meaning. "Oh, that Ashley." Her tone went flat. "Calculus now. Gotta go."

Her abrupt hang-up spoke volumes. The girl was hiding something, and it had to do with Ashley. What could make a teenager who fearlessly rode fast horses be so afraid of a simple conversation?

Nikki's database search showed only one Robart family in the foothills near Mountain View. The address was less than ten miles from the training center, close enough for a teenager to have managed early morning riding duties. Worth the drive.

Afternoon traffic flowed smoothly as Nikki followed the highway toward the foothills, retracing her morning drive. Semi trucks hauled their cargo through the heat, their diesel engines a constant rumble against her windows. She eased over to the inner lane, watching for her exit as shopping centers and tract homes gradually gave way to more rural landscapes.

The Robarts lived in a modest ranch house with a patchy lawn and drawn curtains. A basketball hoop hung over the garage, its net gray and fraying. A scatter of toys suggested younger siblings.

Nikki left Gunner in the car with the air conditioning running. She rang the doorbell, hearing the chaos of children's voices drift from inside, the sound of multiple lives being lived in cramped quarters.

A tired-looking woman answered, wiping her hands on a dishtowel. "Yes?" she asked, clearly wary of unexpected visitors.

"I'm investigating security issues at Mountain View Training Center," Nikki said, showing her PI license. "There've been some incidents recently, and we're talking to people who've spent time there. Is Ashley home from school yet?"

"Ashley? Yes, she's home. Not feeling well today." She shook her head, worry evident beneath her resignation. "She used to be so active. Now she sleeps half the day."

A door slammed somewhere in the house, followed by childish squeals. "Ashley!" the woman called over her shoulder. "Someone to see you."

Moments later, a thin girl appeared in the hall. Baggy sweats hung on her small frame, making her appear even more diminished. Dark circles shadowed her eyes, and her shoulders curved inward, as if trying to make herself invisible. This withdrawn figure bore little resemblance to the "bubbly rider with a lovely seat" that Rachel had described.

"This lady's asking about Mountain View," her mother said.

Ashley's face turned even paler. "I don't ride anymore."

"You were there the day Mr. Turner was hurt," Nikki said gently. "Your statement helped explain what happened."

"I told the police everything." Ashley's voice was barely audible, her eyes fixed on the floor. "Kat's horse spooked, that's all. Nothing more to say."

She turned away, retreating wraithlike down the hall.

"Sorry." Her mother shrugged, her eyes following her daughter. "She's not very social these days. Teenagers, you know. I keep telling her to get out more, maybe go back to the horses." Despite the shrug, worry lined her face. Like many parents, she seemed caught between concern and confusion about her daughter's changes.

Nikki thanked her and returned to her car, Ashley's reaction heavy on her mind. The girl's withdrawal from social life had been obvious. And Kat's evasiveness about Ashley seemed connected. Two teenage girls, both present at the same accident. Kat, still riding at the barn but refusing to discuss her friend. And Ashley, isolated at home yet clinging to her story.

It seemed that whatever happened that October morning went beyond a heartbreaking mishap. And somewhere between their vagueness lay the truth about Jim Turner's accident.

She needed to talk to Kat in person, preferably without Rachel around. The teenager might reveal more if she weren't worried about upsetting her mother. Tomorrow was Saturday, no school to hide behind. There'd be an opportunity to catch Kat after her ride, when Rachel would be busy with Conan. But time with Kat was secondary to the more immediate concern surrounding Mountain View's security.

Conan's vulnerability nagged at her. Rachel and Marco were dedicated but they weren't security professionals. They couldn't anticipate every threat. And Rachel had made it clear that hiring a night guard was financially impossible. Was there something more Nikki could do besides cameras and locked feed rooms? Some other way to protect Conan without a professional security guard? They needed something that would buy them time if—when—the threats escalated.

Wellington was unlikely to come storming into the barn. His actions were more underhanded, like starting drug rumors and sending traffic and sick animals. But things were different in Saudi. Those two men had shown up armed, making direct demands. It was hard to anticipate their next move.

She tapped the steering wheel, trying to be creative. Then she turned her car toward Mountain View. It was only a few minutes' drive away, and there was another step they could take to keep Conan safe. One that wouldn't cost Rachel a dime.

The training facility was quiet when she drove in. Afternoons were clearly a time for horses and stable hands to rest. Nikki slipped past the drowsing cat at the barn entrance and made her way down the shadowed aisle.

Rachel sat in her watch chair beside Conan's stall, alert despite the exhaustion showing in her face. Like most trainers approaching a big race, she probably hadn't slept well in weeks, constantly second-guessing workout schedules, feed programs and equipment choices. But Rachel faced additional challenges: Wellington's smear campaign, limited resources and now actual threats. Marco's soft snores drifted from the tack room, a reminder that at least someone was getting valuable rest.

"You know all the horses here," Nikki said, scanning the row of curious heads hanging over stall doors. "Is there another bay that looks like Conan?"

"Jenny's Quarter Horse, two stalls down. Why?"

"Those Saudi reps weren't horsemen. They probably can't tell one horse from another, not if they're roughly the same color." Nikki met Rachel's gaze. "Let's make it harder to find him."

Understanding brightened Rachel's face, and she scrambled from her chair. "Jenny would do it. She boards here because it's close to the trails, and she can make some extra money ponying."

One quick phone call to Sonny's owner and they were switching horses, haynets and salt licks, keeping movements casual in case anyone was watching. The cameras would still cover Conan's new location, but nighttime visitors would see what they expected: Rachel's chair in front of "his" stall.

"Clever but simple," Rachel said, tucking Marco's thermos beneath the chair. "Though I made it clear Conan wasn't for sale. I doubt those men will return."

"Maybe not," Nikki said, her hand automatically checking where her Glock would normally rest. From now on, she wouldn't leave it behind.

Shadows crept across the aisle as the sun painted jail-like lines between the stalls, transforming the peaceful barn into something more sinister. But the gathering darkness wasn't what troubled her. Men who arrived armed and showing their weapons weren't making idle threats. They were announcing intentions.

And in her experience, they usually had a backup plan. One they'd execute with considerably more force.

CHAPTER ELEVEN

Nikki's phone pierced the darkness, its ring shattering her sleep. The red numbers on her clock read 4:37. She fumbled for her phone, noting Justin's side of the bed was empty. The sheets still held warmth from before his homicide call-out. After a year living together, they'd both grown accustomed to these night departures—his for homicide scenes, hers for surveillance or client emergencies.

"Someone's in the barn!" Rachel's voice cracked with panic before Nikki could even mumble a greeting. Ragged breathing and rustling clothes carried through the phone, accompanying Rachel's frantic words. "The security camera—two men with Sonny. And Marco's not moving. Oh God, he's not moving at all. I called 911, they're on their way."

Nikki hurried to the closet, phone trapped between her ear and shoulder as she pulled on clothes. Her fingers found jeans, a sweater, boots. Gunner appeared at her side, anticipating a quick departure.

"Where are you?" Nikki asked.

"Still at my house. Kat's already in the truck." A door slammed, engine turning over. "We're heading to the barn now."

"I'm on my way," Nikki said, grabbing her Glock from the bedside safe. "Don't touch anything the police might need."

But Rachel had already hung up, leaving Nikki to wonder why her own hidden camera hadn't captured any activity. If the thieves had approached from the far side of the track, bypassing her surveillance, they would face a much longer trek. That route might give police more time to intercept before they disappeared with Sonny.

The quiet freeway stretched ahead as Nikki pushed her car through the darkness. Gunner sat in the back, his expressive eyes mirroring her concern. Even with clear roads, it would take close to ninety minutes to reach the barn. A lot could happen in that time. A lot could already have happened.

Twenty minutes later, her phone lit up with a text from Rachel: *Marco was drugged, conscious but confused. He's in ambulance on way to hospital. Police processing scene.*

Nikki rubbed a hand over her cheek, mind racing. The intruders were professional enough to drug Marco and to move quickly around the property. But not savvy enough to verify that they had the right horse?

Anyone with basic horse experience would have realized Sonny wasn't a Thoroughbred. Where Conan stood over sixteen hands with the lean, long-legged build typical of his breed, Sonny was a compact Quarter Horse with heavier muscles and a shorter back. The difference between a horse bred for explosive quarter-mile sprints versus one created for longer races was as obvious as comparing a linebacker to a marathon runner. The two Saudi men seemed the obvious suspects but she'd clearly overestimated their intelligence. Or underestimated their desperation.

The foothills finally turned visible, their dark outline looming against the horizon. She'd made the drive to Mountain View in record time but already dawn lightened the eastern sky. Wind rustled through the eucalyptus trees lining the road, their shadowed movement deepening the gloom. A patrol car sat by Conan's barn, its light bar ominously rotating, streaking the wall in red and blue.

She scooped up her pack and Gunner's tracking harness. He whined with anticipation as she buckled the straps across his chest and shoulders. This wasn't protection work, this was tracking: his favorite game. She added her Glock to the pack and hurried toward the barn.

Inside, powerful police flashlights created harsh light that emphasized the wrongness of the scene. Dust motes swirled in the disturbed air, caught in their beams. Instead of cheery morning greetings, there were only clipped official voices.

Rachel stood in the aisle, her face ghostly pale. She'd clearly dressed in a hurry—mismatched boots and a jacket thrown over red cotton pajamas printed with tiny horse shoes. A technician photographed Sonny's empty stall while another dusted Marco's overturned chair for prints. The thermos lay tagged on its side where a dark pool of coffee had spread like a stain.

"They drugged Marco's coffee," Rachel said, hands twisting together as she spoke. "Must have done it when he had Conan outside grazing. The ambulance crew said he was conscious but disoriented. They're going to run blood tests."

Sonny's empty stall yawned dark and accusatory while Conan watched the activity from his temporary home, two doors down. He seemed unaffected by the chaos, though several other horses kicked the walls, protesting the change in routine.

The deputy looked up from his notebook, flashlight catching Gunner's reflective harness."Ma'am, this is a crime scene. We have procedures."

"I'm a licensed PI," Nikki said, showing her credentials. "And my dog's certified for tracking. Level Two search and rescue, specialty in air scent."

"We already have a K9 unit responding."

"That could take an hour. My dog's here now." Nikki kept her voice calm. But inside, she was shattered about Sonny and his possible fate. She'd assumed an intruder would be confused about finding a different horse and have to rethink any plan. Hadn't imagined they'd be so dense as to steal the wrong horse.

The deputy hesitated, protocol warring with practicality. Every minute decreased their chances of finding Sonny alive. Horse thieves wouldn't keep the wrong animal long. "Maybe," he said finally. "But I've got to notify my sergeant."

"I want Nikki to try," Rachel said, her voice carrying the firmness that came from years of giving instructions to grooms and exercise riders. "She's the PI who told me to install the surveillance cameras. That's the only reason we even know what happened." The set of her shoulders made it clear this wasn't a request but a decision. Trainers didn't ask permission when it came to their horses. They simply directed what needed to be done.

The officer gave a grudging nod and Nikki quickly turned to Rachel. "I need something of Sonny's. An unwashed saddle pad would be perfect."

Rachel nodded and hurried to the tack room, returning with a sweat-stained blue pad, still bearing the imprint of a saddle. "He used this yesterday," she said.

Nikki held it in front of Gunner, letting him take several deep sniffs. His nostrils flared as he processed the scent, his tail wagging with eagerness.

"Find," she said.

Behind her, the deputy's voice spoke into his radio. "Dispatch, we've got a PI with a tracking dog heading out the east end of the barn. Keep units updated on location."

Voices faded as Nikki turned her full attention to Gunner. They swept out the rear door, into air heavy with dew. His nose stayed low to the ground where multiple prints marked the horse path. His body language showed he had a strong scent—head low, tail straight, muscles taut with purpose.

They sprinted past five barns, their speed drawing curious stares. Grooms gaped over the water hoses and riders pulled up their horses, their usual routines interrupted by the sight of a K9 in tracking gear.

The acrid taste of adrenaline mixed with Nikki's fear for Sonny, and her thudding heart matched the rhythm of her pounding feet. A woman aboard a snorting chestnut called out, asking the reason for the police cars, but Nikki couldn't waste breath answering.

Gunner led her toward the track. The mile-long oval spread before them, already busy with morning training. Horses circled at various speeds, some jogging on the outside while others galloped along the rail. The small grandstand was empty except for a few trainers holding coffee and stopwatches.

Nikki stopped a reluctant Gunner by the gap, pulled out her phone and called the Mountain View office. Jim Turner answered almost immediately.

"Need the track cleared," she said, her breath coming in ragged bursts. "Tracking Jenny's horse."

"The police told me about Sonny." Concern colored Jim's voice, though a subtle undercurrent of irritation leaked through. "Another crisis for you to solve, I see. Give me a minute. And good luck."

The loudspeaker crackled to life, his authoritative voice requesting that the track be cleared. Riders instantly turned their mounts toward the gap. Past "loose horse" warnings and training accidents had conditioned riders to respond to emergency announcements—protecting their charges and themselves from whatever danger might be present.

As soon as the last horse cleared, Nikki and Gunner shot through the gap. Her boots sunk in the freshly harrowed dirt, every step requiring extra effort. Gunner surged ahead, never losing the trail despite the confusing mix of hoof prints. Her breath came in painful gasps. She was fit, but running on the deep track was like wading through water.

Halfway around, where long morning shadows stretched across the oval, Gunner veered toward the red and white pole. Beside it, the outer rail had been smashed. Fresh splinters gleamed against the wood, and prints marked the spot where Sonny had been led over the downed rail and onto the public road.

Two sets of human footprints flanked the horse's trail. Dress shoes, not paddock boots. Men who didn't belong on a track, and who obviously couldn't tell the difference between Sonny and Conan. And it was her fault they'd taken the wrong horse. She'd put Sonny at risk and she had to get him back.

She lengthened her stride on the gravel road, desperation pushing her forward. Ahead, the parking lot spread before them with its wide expanse of crushed stone bordered by eucalyptus trees. But it was empty.

Gunner circled twice, trying to pick up the scent, then stopped, whining with frustration. She pulled his ball from the pack, tossing it to him as a reward. "Good dog," she said.

He caught it with ease, tail wagging with delight. The reward was crucial. K9s needed that positive reinforcement after every search, successful or not, to maintain their enthusiasm for the next challenge. Without it, even the best tracking dogs could lose their drive. Gunner had done everything right, following the trail through conflicting scents. The fact that Sonny was gone wasn't his failure.

But her attention remained fixed on the ground where fresh tire tracks crisscrossed the gravel. A deeper indent showed where a ramp had been lowered. Not a step-up trailer but a larger unit. The kind of professional rig that would make loading a strange horse easier.

Her phone buzzed. She debated answering until she saw who it was.

"Marco's lucid," Rachel said, her voice holding fragile relief. "They're doing preliminary blood work. Police are testing the thermos."

"Good." Nikki said, still eyeing the tire patterns in the parking lot. "They took Sonny in a trailer. Lot is empty."

"Oh, no!" Rachel's voice cracked. "Jenny's on her way. How do I tell her they took her horse because of me?"

"Actually it was because of me." Nikki swallowed back a guilty lump. She'd suggested the stall switch, thinking it would confuse possible thieves. But now an innocent horse was paying the price.

There was a long silence. They both understood the weight of what had happened. A friend's treasured horse had been stolen merely because his owner had been kind enough to help.

"But why take him at all?" Rachel said. "Once they saw it wasn't Conan?"

"I don't think they knew. Which means it wasn't Wellington's people. They'd know Conan, even in the dark."

"It's been light for a while." Fear threaded Rachel's words. "What happens when they realize their mistake?"

Nikki checked her watch, 7:30. By now the thieves would have stopped somewhere quiet, probably a truck stop where a trailer wouldn't draw attention. Maybe they'd already sent photos to their boss. And then a stolen Quarter Horse worth a few thousand dollars would become a liability.

"I'll drive the main roads," she said, already mapping possible routes in her mind. "Check truck stops. Call me if you hear anything."

But she knew finding one trailer in this vast area needed a lot of luck. And Sonny's time might be running out.

CHAPTER TWELVE

The sun had climbed over the horizon, leaving shades of gold and rose. Somewhere on these roads, horse thieves were probably discovering they'd stolen the wrong animal. Nikki gripped the steering wheel, trying not to picture their reaction. Criminals didn't keep mistakes around long, especially four-legged ones. She guessed she had maybe an hour before they decided to cut their losses with a bullet.

She lowered all four windows, her fingers white-knuckled on the wheel. Cold air rushed through the car, carrying hints of sage from the surrounding hills. The fresh air would help Gunner's tracking abilities, though it made her shiver.

In the back seat, his nose twitched as he sorted through the web of morning scents—diesel exhaust from passing trucks, grease from roadside restaurants, manure from livestock yards. One whiff of Sonny's distinctive smell and he'd alert, if only she could get close enough.

The thieves had taken Sonny at 4:30 am, spent roughly twenty-five minutes walking him halfway around the track and loading up. By now, even with highway trailer restrictions, they'd covered at least sixty miles. Enough distance to make the search feel impossible.

She pushed away her pessimism. They might not be too far ahead. Wouldn't want to risk busy highways and weigh stations.

They'd prefer a quiet place to verify their cargo. Then deal with their mistake.

She pressed the accelerator, deciding to drive another forty miles before checking the sides of the road. Her police scanner crackled with routine calls. But there were no alerts about abandoned horses. Or dead ones.

Half an hour later, she pulled into a gas station, one big enough to handle multiple rigs. The parking lot stretched wide, filled with semis and horse trailers, the usual morning traffic heading to shows and sales. Gunner stuck his head out the window, his nose quivering as he sorted through smells. But he showed little interest, and she rolled back onto the highway.

Her throat felt impossibly dry and she kept swallowing. She'd tracked missing people, stolen property and lost pets. But this felt different. She'd been the one to suggest switching stalls. And every passing minute increased the likelihood that the thieves would choose the easiest solution. They'd probably checked in with their boss by now. The question was how they'd be instructed to handle it.

Please don't hurt him. But the stubborn lump stuck in her throat. Wellington might be vindictive, but he was a horseman. He'd be loath to harm an innocent animal. The Saudis though... Their idea of acceptable collateral damage might be different.

The next truck stop sprawled across several acres, busy even at this hour. Gunner stuck his head out the window as she cruised past rows of rigs. But he didn't alert to anything. A horse trailer caught her eye but it was the wrong size. Another fit the size but had the wrong type of ramp. Her heart jumped at each trailer, dropped with each disappointment. Every empty parking lot felt like a nail in Sonny's coffin. And the sun kept climbing, time slipping away.

Her phone buzzed. Rachel. Pulling in a hopeful breath, she activated the hands-free. "Any news?"

"Marco's being sent home," Rachel said. "They found GHB in his system but he'll be fine. Won't stop blaming himself though. Jenny's here," she added. "Police want a statement from her, but..." She didn't need to finish. The hitching sobs in the background said enough.

"What are the authorities doing?" Nikki forced her voice to steady while trying to block the sounds of Jenny's anguish.

"Put out a BOLO for the trailer. But they're saying without a license plate, it's ineffective." Rachel's frustration carried through the phone. "And they're pulling footage from all the public cameras near Mountain View."

Nikki checked her mirrors, changing lanes to pass a slow-moving truck. "Did the police talk to Wellington?"

"Yes, he's been in Kentucky since Thursday. Seemed stunned that I even thought he'd be responsible for stealing a horse, let alone the wrong one. Sounded genuinely sad to hear about Sonny."

The lump in Nikki's throat grew. If Wellington wasn't behind this, that left the Saudis. And she had no experience with their way of thinking, the value they'd put on a friendly riding horse.

"I'm heading north," she said, spotting signs for another truck stop ahead. "Some big rest areas up this way. Gunner will let me know if he catches a scent."

"Be careful," Rachel said. "These men—"

She broke off as a woman's voice murmured something in the background. "Jenny wants to know if you've checked any livestock lots. Places where they might have left him."

"Not yet." Nikki softened her tone. "I'm still hopeful they're just ahead of me."

"The police think they're probably heading toward Mexico," Rachel said. "That they might have stolen a bunch of horses for m-meat."

"Doubt they went that way," Nikki said, pulling into another sprawling truck stop, this one bustling with traffic. Eighteen-wheelers idled in neat rows while drivers clutching coffee cups hurried between the restaurant and their rigs. Horse trailers of various sizes occupied the far section, temporary rest stops for animals being hauled to shows, sales and races across the state. "They'll want to unload their mistake as quickly as possible," she added. "Not drive any distance. Let me check this place."

She ended the call and circled the large parking area. A gleaming aluminum trailer sat alone in the back lot, parked suspiciously far from the pumps. Hope rose as she drove closer and confirmed it was a ramp load. From inside, a horse nickered, as if in protest. She stepped out, took a picture of the plate then hurried to the side of the truck.

A driver rounded the front bumper, steam rising from his coffee cup, cowboy hat set at a jaunty angle. His easy stride faltered at the sight of someone so close to his rig. "Help you, ma'am?"

Nikki noted the show ribbons proudly displayed in his cab window and forced a casual smile. "Sorry to bother you. Looking for a friend's trailer."

He nodded sympathetically. "Lot of us out early. Good luck finding your friend."

Back in the car, Nikki slammed her palm against the steering wheel. Another dead end, and precious minutes ticking away. Maybe she'd guessed wrong about their route. If they chose to avoid cameras and weigh stations, that left the secondary routes through the foothills. Slower driving but places where a horse could disappear.

She veered onto the secondary road, passing ranch houses and small acreages with grazing horses that bore little resemblance to Sonny. The mountain road twisted through stands of pine and scrub oak, its crumbling shoulder barely wide enough for a car, let alone a trailer. Not that they'd stop on this section. A drop-off would be too visible. And people would investigate a gunshot. But there were occasional turnarounds, along with old logging roads and trailheads that accessed the foothills.

She pulled up a tracking grid on the GPS, dividing the search area into quadrants based on the thieves' likely speed and fuel range. Three routes connected back to the highway, but only the northern fork offered the required coverage to dump a horse without being seen. She marked the turnouts and fire roads, calculating drive times against sunrise. If they'd wanted anonymity, this twenty-mile stretch was an ideal spot.

She turned on her four-way flashers, her gaze shifting from the road to the rearview mirror, keeping a close eye on Gunner. His head was out the window, nose quivering as he sorted through layers of scent: fertilizer, gas, livestock and a multitude of other odors too faint for her nose.

A car roared past, horn blaring. She ignored it, continuing to crawl along as she eyed the dirt roads branching into the trees. Each turnoff presented a choice for the thieves. Let Sonny loose? He could cause an accident and draw unwanted attention. Take time to hide him properly? Risk being seen.

And the final option—the one she hated to consider—was that they walked him into a scrub-filled ditch and shot him. He might not be noticed for days. There would be little media attention. Horse theft happened. She knew which option most professionals would choose.

She continued inching along, wavering between hopelessness and forced optimism. Just as she neared another fire road, Gunner's head snapped up. His breathing changed to the short, focused sniffs she knew so well: He'd caught something on the crosswinds. After hundreds of searches together, she recognized this buildup to an alert. Then he gave a distinctive bark, followed by his sit that meant absolute certainty.

She swerved onto the shoulder, crunching gravel beneath her tires. Her hands shook as she clipped on Gunner's leash and grabbed her gun. He hadn't reacted to any of the grazing horses they'd passed, and he rarely made a false alert. It had to be Sonny. But was he alive?

Gunner strained forward, barely giving her time to lock the car and pocket her keys. The road curved into dense forest, perfect cover for disposing of evidence. Or a body.

Sucking in a fortifying breath she followed Gunner's taut lead. Pine needles muffled their steps as they moved along the road. Every swaying branch made her tense, looking for Sonny or his lifeless body. The deeper they went, the more her stomach twisted.

A nicker drifted through the trees, so faint she thought it came from an adjacent acreage. But Gunner's tail wagged and he sped up. The path curved between two large pines then emerged in a sun-dappled clearing. And for a moment she quit breathing.

There stood Sonny, tied to a tree, looking for all the world as if he was just waiting for his rider.

"Oh thank God." Her knees buckled and she blinked hard, half-expecting him to disappear. But he remained solid and real, even as she hurried to him.

Her hands shook as she ran them over his legs and flanks, checking for injuries, finding nothing but warm, healthy horse.

The clearing had been well chosen, hidden from the road but accessible enough for a trailer. Tire tracks suggested they'd backed in and unloaded. No signs of struggle or panic. These weren't amateurs dealing with a mind-boggling problem.

"Good dog, Gunner," she said, sharing her attention between dog and horse, praising Gunner for his wonderful nose and Sonny for being so cooperative. If he had been a different sort, the outcome might not have been as happy. Even non-horsemen would have appreciated that Sonny was an obliging gentleman.

She untied him, noting that it wasn't a quick-release but a precise bowline. And the rope was new. Someone had come prepared. They could have shot Sonny, left his body where it might never be found. Instead, they'd chosen this sheltered spot, making sure he was safe and secure.

Sonny lowered his head, eager to munch on the grass. Nikki pulled out her phone, blinking with gratitude as she called Rachel. "We found him. He's fine."

Rachel's relieved sob carried through the phone along with several ecstatic cheers in the background. Kat and Jenny, no doubt.

"Really?" Rachel asked. "He's okay?"

"Not a scratch on him. He's eating grass right now. Gunner found him tied to a tree about sixty miles north of the training center. He'll need a ride home."

"I'll ask Jim to arrange a trailer," Rachel said. "He knows everyone in the area. Can you stay with him? I'll have the driver call you for directions."

"We'll be right here." Nikki ended the call and settled against the trunk of a young oak, its bark rough through her jacket. Sun filtered through the branches, creating shifting patterns on the ground. Gunner explored the clearing, occasionally pausing to toss and catch his ball. His relaxed play showed no threats lurked. And Sonny grazed contentedly, as if being stolen by strangers and abandoned in the woods was a normal occurrence.

The tight band around her chest gradually loosened. They'd won this round. Sonny was safe, Marco would recover and their stall-switching plan had actually worked. Sort of. But that bowline was revealing. No horseman would use it. They all learned quick-release knots their first day around horses. This was something else entirely, a precise knot favored by military or maritime professionals.

These weren't common thieves and definitely not Wellington's people. Someone had given orders to steal a specific horse, and they'd executed the job with precision. Yet when they'd realized their mistake, they'd chosen mercy over expedience. The clearing's location, the new rope, the secure knot—all suggested planning and professionalism rather than panic. Thankfully they'd taken the time to ensure Sonny's safety even while knowing their mission had failed.

She tightened her jacket, new fears leaving her chilled. Because next time they wouldn't make the same mistake. Next time they'd verify their target. And next time, they might not be so merciful.

CHAPTER THIRTEEN

━━━━◦━━━━

Back in his regular stall, Sonny munched happily on a flake of Conan's premium alfalfa while Jenny groomed every inch of him, for the third time. "Good boy," she kept murmuring as she moved the brush over his neck. "Such a good, brave boy."

Nikki doubted Sonny had any idea of the extent of his adventure, but his calm attitude had probably saved his life. Thieves didn't like complications, and an unruly horse would have been a liability.

She held Conan in the aisle while Rachel adjusted his girth and stretched out his front legs. "You know where he's safest?" Rachel said to Nikki. "Out on the track. No one can catch him there. And where the heck is Kat? She should be helping me, not you."

"I'll see if she's outside," Nikki said, passing Rachel the reins. She was happy to help, knowing that Marco's absence had disrupted the usual routine. But the sound of an idling car grabbed her attention. With all that had happened, she wanted to check every vehicle that stopped by Conan's barn.

She moved to the barn entrance, Gunner at her side, and spotted Jim's van. The hydraulic lift whirred as it lowered his wheelchair. Kat stood beside the open van, her stiff arms radiating tension. Though the gusty breeze scattered their words, her body language spoke volumes. This appeared to be more than typical teen defiance.

Jim leaned forward, gesturing. Kat shook her head, whirled and rushed into the barn, barely acknowledging Nikki as she passed. Her cheeks flamed and she closed the buckle of her helmet with a sharp click.

"Ready?" Rachel called, holding Conan's reins, seeming oblivious to her daughter's emotion.

Kat nodded, stepping closer so her mother could leg her into the saddle. She straightened, tightening the reins too quickly. Conan jigged in protest but quickly settled when she gave his neck an apologetic pat.

"Just an easy jog," Rachel said. "We'll do his final work tomorrow. Everyone's schedule is off after this morning's drama."

Kat gave another wordless nod. Her eyes were fixed straight ahead, not looking at the man in the wheelchair rolling through the front entrance. She and Conan disappeared through the back door, her spine poker stiff, every movement showing her desire to escape the barn. And her ex-stepfather.

Jim stopped near Rachel and Nikki, his expression concerned. "Guess it's time to talk about security. I heard Marco's out for at least two days, and you can't sit up all night. I can assign my guard to this barn. He'll handle eight to eight. No charge."

Rachel jammed her hands in her pockets, shaking her head. "Jim, we can't—"

"This isn't about us. After what happened with Sonny, it's clear these people mean business. I won't have any person or animal hurt, or worse, on my property. Once he's at Santa Anita you'll have track security. That's what, six days?"

His voice softened. "Please, Rachel. Let me help. I'm offering twelve hours of professional coverage. Rolf is armed and extremely capable. Marco can sleep, build up his strength. And you can train your horse without worrying that someone might steal him in the middle of the night."

A current of emotions ran beneath their words. For all their problems, Jim clearly still cared about Rachel. And he'd come through earlier this morning, quickly clearing the track and also finding a trailer to bring Sonny home. He ran an efficient facility. No wonder there was a wait list.

"I'm heading over to watch Conan," Nikki said, guessing they'd prefer privacy to work out any arrangement. Rachel obviously didn't want to accept any favors from Jim, while the set of his jaw showed he was equally determined to help.

Besides, this was a good chance to ask Kat about Ashley Robart and what really happened with Conan and Jim. The teenager might open up without anyone else around.

She and Gunner followed the horse path toward the track. The oval was quiet this late in the morning. Only a few horses walked along the outer rail while Conan and Kat circled at an easy jog. Kat looked relaxed now, her hands quiet on the reins.

A whiff of perfume signaled a feminine visitor. Sophia Mendez approached, her stilettos navigating the dirt with practiced ease. Her cream blouse, tailored slacks and swinging silver earrings left Nikki feeling underdressed. But beneath Sophia's polished appearance and the salon-fresh highlights, her expression held a mix of irritation and concern.

"Have you seen Jim?" she asked, her casual question at odds with her expression.

"Yes, he's in the barn talking to Rachel."

"About security? I hope he's not offering our night guard," Sophia snapped. "Rolf is already patrolling six barns as well as the office."

"I'm not sure what arrangements they're making." Nikki realized she wasn't the only one who'd noticed Jim's interest in his ex. "But Rachel needs help after what happened to Sonny."

Sophia's lips tightened. "Rachel's very capable. She doesn't need Jim's help. And I know for a fact Kat doesn't want it either."

"Oh?" Nikki widened her eyes, hoping the woman would keep talking.

"I know Kat well. She was always mean to Jim, even before the divorce. I think that's what came between him and Rachel. Her bad attitude.

"He'd try to give her riding tips," Sophia went on. "But she'd never listen. And she always had some stupid reason why she couldn't help him in the office." She glanced across the track to where Kat and Conan moved as a team. "Now she acts like she owns the place just because her mother trains one good horse."

Sophia gave a scornful sniff. "I don't understand why Jim wants to stay friends with Rachel considering Kat won't give him the time of day. It's not fair. *He* should be the one who's mad. We should never have let that horse come back. And I'll keep telling him that until he listens."

She spun away, heels stabbing the dirt. It was notable she didn't head to Conan's barn. Instead, she stalked back to the office, as if unwilling to see Rachel and Jim together. Or force an argument. Nikki wasn't sure of the dynamics. However the woman's reaction suggested complications ahead. Clearly Jim's desire to help Rachel had stirred up more than just security concerns.

But that wasn't her concern, and watching a horse like Conan quickly lifted Nikki's spirits. Even at an easy jog, the horse moved with controlled power, Kat keeping him well in hand. Ten minutes later, they headed off the track, where Nikki met them at the gap.

"He felt great, so focused," Kat said. "Not affected by the chaos this morning." Her eyes darted along the path. "Is Jim still in the barn? With Mom?"

The question carried weight beyond simple curiosity. Even with Conan moving like a dream, Kat's guard never seemed to drop when it came to her former stepfather.

"I think he's still there," Nikki said. "He offered his watchman for night security."

Kat groaned, glancing down at Nikki as if looking for agreement. "She shouldn't have anything to do with him. Not after everything. She can't ever take him back!"

"Because of what happened? Maybe something with Ashley?"

Kat's face went blank and almost immediately Conan's stride lengthened, as if he sensed his rider's need to escape. "I have to cool him out. And the sun's too hot now."

"Wait," Nikki said, keeping pace with the accelerating horse. "If something happened that day, knowing about it might help protect Conan. Anything you tell me stays confidential. I don't work for the insurance company or the police. I work for your mother. My job is keeping you all safe, not exposing secrets."

"Nothing happened," Kat muttered. "Conan spooked, that's all. And it has nothing to do with Ashley."

Moments later all Nikki could see were Conan's powerful hindquarters as his ground-eating walk carried Kat away. Her barriers were back up, but her reaction revealed plenty. Both teens carried a secret that went far beyond a spooked horse. And somehow Jim was at its core.

Nikki stood rooted in place, a hollow feeling spreading in her chest. The girl's rigid posture struck a chord. Her own teenage years—those months on the streets looking for Erin—had taught her more about self-preservation than any PI course ever could. She knew firsthand that kids didn't maintain this kind of wall unless the stakes were desperately high.

Kat wasn't protecting herself. The way she reacted to Jim and her instant shutdown at Ashley's name weren't the reactions of someone hiding their own mistakes. That was the defensive stance of someone shielding others. The question was: Who was she trying to protect? Her mother? Ashley? Or maybe even Conan?

CHAPTER FOURTEEN

The stillness of Nikki's office was jarring after the morning's chaos at Mountain View. She'd left the center with more questions than answers—Kat's evasiveness, Sophia's obvious jealousy and Jim's determined helpfulness with a horse he seemed to hate. All the contradictions circled each other like wary fighters, the pattern between them hard to grasp.

She turned to her computer, fingers punching the keyboard as she researched insurance coverage for equestrian facilities. Standard policies included one million maximum liability with additional riders for property damage, employee injury and business interruption. Even larger facilities rarely exceeded liability coverage beyond two million.

She'd investigated insurance fraud before and couldn't help being suspicious. Maybe Jim had done something around Conan that would nullify coverage. Maybe the two girls had witnessed it, and he was influencing them to keep quiet. She knew Jim was waiting on a payout but she had no idea how much. Insurance might not even be a factor. But she had to keep digging.

She picked up her phone and called Rachel. "Can you tell me what company insures Mountain View?"

"Westward Mutual," Rachel said. "Jim's been with them since I first started boarding. He spends a fortune on premiums."

Perfect. Rachel's new openness made everything easier. Nikki thanked her and ended the call. She pulled up the Westward Mutual website and found the direct line to their claims division. Clearing her throat, she pressed in the number.

"This is Jessica Mills with Mountain View security," she said, adopting her most professional tone. "In light of a recent incident, I'm reviewing our coverage regarding stolen animals."

"Yes, we heard about what happened today," the agent said. "Quite concerning after Mr. Turner's accident claim. Which is why we've had to limit coverage." The man's voice turned defensive. "You have to understand that his five-million payout will classify the facility as a high-risk client. That means a ten thousand dollar cap on any stolen horse." The agent went on about qualifying security upgrades but Nikki had heard enough and ended the call.

She leaned back in her chair, staring at the screen—Jim was about to receive five million dollars. There'd be no need for any more GoFundMe campaigns, and she wondered if Rachel knew the extent of his payout. Nikki called her back.

"Yes, he's due a payout," Rachel confirmed. "He's hopeful it will come through soon. I'm not sure of the amount."

"I heard it was five million."

Rachel's quick intake of breath showed her surprise. "Really? That's quite a lot. He's talked of selling but maybe now he won't have to. Maybe he'll be able to repay those generous people who made donations."

"Maybe," Nikki said, without much conviction.

"And truthfully I know he'd rather be able to walk than receive any amount of money."

"I'm sure that's true." Nikki's voice softened. Some things couldn't be measured in dollars, no matter how many zeros followed the number. "Thanks for the information, Rachel. I'll let you know if I find anything important."

She ended the call, turning back to her computer screen and its pages of financial records and insurance forms. Jim's accident had changed everything at Mountain View—relationships, finances and even the future of the facility. Whether the changes were leading somewhere better or worse remained to be seen.

Her news alert pinged. She clicked the link and felt her throat close. A new blog post about Conan, and it was already gathering comments.

***VIOLENCE FOLLOWS DERBY CONTENDER* by Mike Jensen Racing Insider Blog**

The fairy-tale story of Conan's rise from outlaw to Derby contender has taken a darker turn. After paralyzing a man and injuring gate crew members, the controversial colt's presence at Mountain View Training Center sparked new violence this morning.

Sources say two men drugged and assaulted groom and night watchman Marco Sanchez while attempting to steal the horse. In a twist of fate, they took the wrong animal—a woman's Quarter Horse that was later found abandoned.

"This situation has become more than a racing issue," warns a veteran security consultant who requested anonymity. "When millions of dollars and reputations are at stake, people make desperate choices. In my experience, it's only a matter of time before someone else ends up hurt."

With the Santa Anita Derby days away and tension mounting at Mountain View, many wonder when the next tragedy will strike. As one source noted, "Sometimes people die. And in the horse world, accidents happen every day."

Sources close to the investigation express similar concerns. "We've seen escalating violence: first physical assault, then drugging. The next incident could be fatal. Is a horse really worth someone's life?"

Nikki stared at her screen, jaw so tight she could feel her teeth clench. The timing was suspicious, barely hours after Sonny's rescue. Someone had fed Jensen this story, complete with anonymous quotes and manufactured concern.

Jensen's blogs reeked of character assassination. First destroy Conan's reputation, then Rachel's credibility. Create just enough fear that no one would question a tragic accident. But where was all this coming from? She doubted the Saudis would have a blog writer on speed dial. Or if they even cared about public perception.

She stabbed in Jensen's number. "You got your story up fast," she said, once he answered.

"Good afternoon to you too, Nikki." Amusement crept into his voice.

She rose, pacing a circle in her office. "How'd you get the details about Marco being drugged? That was remarkably quick, even for you."

"Something wrong with my facts?" Keyboard clicks carried through the line. He was probably already working on his next story.

"It reads like a hit piece." She stopped in front of the framed photo on her office wall—her sister Erin astride a sleek white-faced bay, smiling at the camera. The last picture taken before she disappeared.

Nikki had missed the signs back then, too young to recognize the patterns of abuse. She wouldn't miss them now. Not when her instincts screamed that someone was constructing a narrative, planning their moves, much like Erin's killer.

"Did Wellington feed this to you?"

"You know I protect my sources." Jensen's tone remained neutral, the voice of someone used to dancing around questions. "And I've been in the business long enough to verify information. Be assured they have intimate knowledge of the situation."

Nikki sat back down, forcing herself to stay calm. "So someone at Mountain View fed you this."

"Nice try. But they were quite clear about anonymity." Jensen paused. "Seemed genuinely worried about where this is heading."

"Worried? Or laying the groundwork for a cover story?"

"Interesting take," Jensen said. "You think there's more here?"

"I think someone could be setting the stage. All these anonymous quotes." She picked up a pen, rolling it in her fingers, carefully choosing her words. "Your blog is well respected, now. I'd hate to see it used to justify something nefarious."

"If you have evidence of a different story, I'm listening." The keyboard clicks in the background stopped.

"Not yet." Nikki dropped the pen, watching it roll across her desk. "But timing like this can't be coincidental. First Wellington's warnings, then escalating violence, now hints of potential accidents."

"Keep me posted." Jensen's tone suggested he'd caught her meaning. "I don't like being played."

She ended the call, the blog's quote about accidents stuck in her mind. Someone seemed to be laying groundwork. But for what?

She pulled the insurance policy back up again, searching for connections between seemingly separate events: Jim's pending settlement, the horse theft that reinforced Conan's "dangerous" reputation and a carefully crafted story warning about potential deaths. Three different incidents around Conan, all pointing in the same troubling direction.

Rachel's comment about Jim trying to hang on to the property was also a red flag. She opened several real estate databases, eventually finding what she'd suspected. An active listing for Mountain View Training Center: *Rare opportunity: 160 acres with premier equestrian facilities including one-mile training track. Recently upgraded ADA-compliant living quarters and office space. Zoned for possible development. Prime location near expanding residential areas. $12.5 million.*

The listing had been posted three weeks ago, hidden in commercial real estate channels where Rachel wouldn't see it. The timing explained Jim's sudden interest in facility security. A violent incident could tank the sale price.

The stakes were mounting: five-million-dollar insurance payout pending, twelve-million-dollar property listing, and now planted stories about inevitable violence that might prevent Conan from racing. The potential losses were staggering, for both Jim and Rachel.

Nikki opened a new file on her laptop. MOUNTAIN VIEW TIMELINE:

Jim purchases 5M insurance policy (date unknown). Rachel files for divorce. Conan arrives at facility. Accident occurs. Ashley Parker witnesses, disappears. Kat defensive about details. Settlement pending. Property listed for sale. Marco drugged, Sonny stolen. Blog appears within hours.

Her fingers hovered over the keyboard. Kat also turned evasive whenever Ashley was mentioned. The teenager was clearly protecting her mother from Jim's renewed interest. But she might also be protecting a friend.

Nikki picked up her phone again, this time calling Justin. It went directly to voice mail. Not unexpected. "Need a favor," she said, leaving a recording. "Can you pull the original police report on Jim Turner's accident? I need to see Ashley Robart's official statement."

She ended the call, tilting forward in her chair as she studied the timeline. The critical pieces were there but gaps remained. Even so, a growing certainty settled in her gut. The blog post wasn't just designed to destroy Conan's career. It was laying the foundation for something much darker. With Conan as the catalyst.

CHAPTER FIFTEEN

Early morning traffic flowed smoothly as Nikki followed the highway toward Mountain View. Semi trucks hauled their cargo through the darkness, creating red rivers of light. She eased into an outer lane, her thoughts on Conan.

After days of constant worry, she looked forward to watching his final work. This case had consumed her thoughts. The stall switch, the cameras, the detailed security plans—all of it circled through her mind on an endless loop. If everything went well today, he'd ship to Santa Anita tomorrow, where track security would take over much of the burden she'd been carrying.

Gunner dozed in the back as she passed landmarks that were becoming familiar. Her headlights caught snapshots of activity, the working world coming awake while most people slept. A vet clinic's neon sign flickered to life, a feed truck rumbled past and a horse trailer labored in the slow lane. These quiet hours were filled with those who dealt with animals, who recognized that they operated on their own internal clocks, indifferent to human convenience.

Her phone buzzed with a text from Justin: *Got that accident report. Sending now.*

She waited for a red light then clicked the file. Ashley Robart's witness statement filled her screen: *I had just galloped a horse and was giving him a bath by the side of the barn. Mr. Turner was near the barn too, heading along the horse path ahead of Kat and Conan.*

Conan was walking quietly but something spooked him. Maybe my horse. There was shouting but by the time I turned around, Mr. Turner was on the ground. It wasn't anyone's fault, just a terrible accident.

The statement felt cautious, as if trying not to point blame. Too careful for a teenage girl describing unexpected trauma, especially the sentence that it wasn't anyone's fault. Maybe Ashley was trying to make sure the insurance company covered Jim's claim. Or maybe she was protecting Kat, emphasizing that Conan wasn't dangerous and that Kat was a competent rider.

The light turned green. Nikki forwarded the report to her office computer for closer study. Right now she wanted to focus on Conan's work. The morning had that special feeling of anticipation that came before an important race. Despite the threats and complications, they were nearly there. Conan would make it to the Santa Anita Derby after all. There was satisfaction in that, a sense of mission accomplished. After today, he'd be safely stabled at the track and she could step back from her role as guardian.

After another thirty minutes of driving, she turned onto the training center's dirt road. Even at this early hour there was extra activity around the grandstand, along with Jim's van parked close to Conan's barn. Further down the road, a reporter lurked, camera ready.

She parked and opened her door, pausing as a uniformed figure approached.

Good morning, ma'am," he said. Close up, she could see the faint scar along his jaw, the tanned and weathered face of someone used to working outdoors. "I'm Rolf Olsen. Mr. Turner mentioned that you and your K9 would be coming by."

He positioned himself where he could see her and the road, his manner both professional and courteous. "Reporters tried getting in earlier," he added. "Mr. Turner wants them directed to the grandstand area instead. But you and your dog are welcome anywhere on the property."

Nikki nodded appreciation as she motioned for Gunner to jump out and then locked her car.

"He's a beauty," Rolf said, dropping to one knee and introducing himself to Gunner. His fingers found the sweet spot behind her dog's left ear. Nikki gaped as Gunner leaned into his touch. She'd never seen him accept a strange man so quickly, let alone show such trust.

"Malinois handler, back in the service," Rolf explained, his face softening as Gunner pressed against his leg.

"Good to have you watching Conan," Nikki said, impressed by the man's quiet competence. "Was everything good last night?"

"Absolutely," Rolf said, straightening. "Conan slept like a baby, flat out in the straw. Seems to know he needs to save energy for something big."

Nikki released a breath she hadn't realized she'd been holding. Not only was this man competent but he also seemed to understand horses. He definitely understood dogs. Gunner's ears drooped when Rolf moved out on the road to check another vehicle, his disappointed whine making it clear he'd have preferred more attention from his new friend.

She headed toward the barn where excited laughter drifted through the doorway, charging the atmosphere. With Rolf watching over things, Nikki also felt a new lightness.

"Glad you could make it!" Rachel called to her from Conan's stall, her face bright with anticipation. "Perfect track conditions. Jim just had it harrowed."

Rachel continued tacking up Conan, smoothing his saddle pad before positioning the saddle on his back. Her movements showed years of experience, the kind of muscle memory that came from thousands of early mornings. Though she clearly missed Marco's help, she moved with the confidence of someone who'd done this job on her own for many years.

Jim had been joking with Rachel but offered Nikki a curt nod that carried none of the warmth he'd just shown his ex-wife. Sophia stood behind his wheelchair, her frown revealing her displeasure at their growing closeness. Similarly, there was no mistaking Jim's attitude shift when Nikki appeared.

It was odd, his dislike. Maybe it was simply her position as an outsider. Or maybe deep down, he wanted something to happen to Conan. He certainly seemed to have a high regard for Rachel. Whatever the reason, Nikki filed away this awareness, another piece in the complicated tensions surrounding the center's star resident.

"Weather's holding too," Jim said, his attention focused on Rachel. "Same forecast for race day. I had them harrow it similar to Santa Anita. Soft cushion, slightly firm on top."

He gestured in the direction of the oval, pride evident in his voice. "Same moisture content, same sand-to-clay ratio. Lets him get used to what he'll feel under his feet on Saturday."

Nikki recognized the advantage he was giving Rachel. Track surfaces could make or break a performance. Every horse had different preferences. Some excelled on firm dirt, some wet, and others preferred it deeper with more cushion. By simulating Santa

Anita's distinctive surface, Jim was offering Conan the perfect final prep.

"You always had a gift for simulating track surfaces," Rachel said, favoring him with a smile that left her green eyes sparkling. The kind of smile that spoke of shared history and forgotten grievances.

Sophia's fingers tightened around the back of Jim's wheelchair as Jim and Rachel enthusiastically discussed track biases. For a moment, they looked like the team they'd once been, two horse people sharing their passion.

Gunner's ears pricked, and Nikki followed his gaze. A reporter had slipped into the barn, camera raised. Before Nikki could move, Rolf materialized in the doorway.

"Sir, this is private property." Rolf's voice was quiet but carried authority. "I'll have to ask you to return to the grandstand area."

"Just need some background color—" The reporter's protest died as Rolf leveled him with a hard look. "Right. Grandstand. Got it."

Nikki shot Rolf an appreciative smile. No drama, no confrontation, just quiet authority. Jim had chosen well.

"Mom?" Kat emerged from the tack room, her voice cutting through the barn's warmth. Her helmet and protective vest were secured and her body language screamed tension as she stopped well back from Jim.

"Can we get going?" she asked, shifting from foot to foot while she waited for Rachel to lead Conan into the aisle.

Nikki noted how Kat's gaze darted everywhere except toward Jim and Sophia. This wasn't the focused concentration of a rider preparing for a critical work, ready to absorb the trainer's instructions. Instead, her attention ping-ponged, as if she were looking for the nearest escape route.

Rachel turned away and bridled Conan. She led him from the stall, positioning him in the center of the aisle. "Good timing," she said, legging Kat into the saddle. "Jim has arranged for the track to be empty."

Kat's expression suggested timing wasn't her concern. Whatever was building between her mother and ex-stepfather, she clearly wasn't happy about it. Neither was Sophia, whose manicured fingers had a vise-like grip on Jim's wheelchair.

"I'll have to drive the van around to watch," Jim said. "The horse path is too deep for my wheels."

"And you shouldn't get too close to that brute," Sophia said. "Not again. We can't risk another accident."

Jim tensed and the momentary flash in his eyes suggested this wasn't the first time he'd resented her controlling tone. But Rachel seemed completely oblivious to the comment. She led Conan down the aisle and out the back door, her focus on the horse. And Kat sat perfectly balanced, hands quiet on the reins. For both women, the world had narrowed to Conan and his upcoming work. Everything else was simply background clutter.

A grin tugged at Nikki's mouth as she and the guard followed them along the horse path. The Parker women's complete dismissal of the drama behind them was delightful—neither had given Sophia's comment a second thought, tuning out relationship complications with a singular focus.

"Fresher air out here," Rolf said, catching her grin and acknowledging the emotional minefield they'd just left. He scanned the opening of every barn they passed, nodding at a few people but maintaining his awareness.

She trailed a relaxed hand over Gunner's head. For the first time in days, she didn't feel it was necessary to check every shadow or passing vehicle. Not with Rolf assigned to watch Conan. "Have you worked here long?" she asked.

"Nine months," Rolf said. "Jumped at the chance. Way better than working the mall. Plus it includes sleeping quarters in the big barn."

"So you know Jim Turner quite well?"

"Not really." Rolf's expression remained pleasant, but something in his eyes shifted—the professional distance of someone who understood boundaries.

Worth a try, Nikki thought, respecting the man even more.

"My father worked at Del Mar back in the eighties," Rolf said, pausing by the gap and positioning himself where he could see both Conan and the grandstand. "I enjoy the animals, keeping them safe. Though today is more about watching people than horses."

Nikki let his comment settle. He might have been referring to the reporters. But no doubt he'd picked up on the complex dynamics playing out between horse and humans, including his boss.

They fell into watchful silence as Kat gathered her reins and Rachel slipped off the lead line. "Don't let him roll until the ¾ pole," Rachel said. "Save him for the race."

Kat nodded and guided Conan to the outside rail for his warm-up, the colt's stride strong but controlled. Rachel's eyes never left the pair. She held her stopwatch loosely, years of training evident in her posture.

Rolf remained between Nikki and the scattering of watchers gathered on the grandstand. His hand rested casually near his hip where she guessed he carried a concealed weapon. The only vehicle by the rail was Jim's white van, now parked at the top of the stretch for a perfect view.

Nikki turned her attention to Conan, satisfied that Rolf was monitoring the spectators. He'd be off duty at eight, but by then Conan would be safely back in his stall. For the next few minutes, she could simply appreciate the horse in motion. There was something hypnotic about watching him gallop, a reminder of why so many people fell in love with horses.

Kat let her reins out a notch and Conan's stride lengthened, his acceleration effortless. This was an athlete in his prime, doing what he loved. By the time he hit the quarter pole, he was in full stride, changing leads smoothly and running straight.

He crossed the finish line with Rachel checking her stop watch. "Twenty-three flat," she said, her voice lifting with excitement.

Conan swept around the turn, galloping out strong, Kat almost motionless in the saddle. This was what made Thoroughbreds special. That eye-catching combination of speed and grace, centuries of breeding distilled into courageous athletic power.

"Just the work I wanted." Rachel pocketed her stopwatch, smiling with relief at Nikki and Rolf. "He came into this so calm. Nice job catching that photographer before he could spook Conan with his flash."

"Part of the job," Rolf said.

"Tomorrow afternoon he ships to Santa Anita," Rachel said. "But I hate to lose your watchful eye. You seem to understand horses."

"Being around them is the best part," he said. "Though right now my focus is making sure you all can get some rest tonight. Jim has given me instructions never to leave Conan's barn so don't worry. I'll even sing some lullabies if it helps him sleep."

Rachel laughed, much more relaxed now that Conan had finished his work. She seemed to appreciate that she was surrounded by people who understood both security needs as well as the quiet pride of a small stable. Conan just had to stay happy and healthy until Saturday, with limited exercise until the race.

Nikki understood her relief. The trainer's hard work was done. Now that Jim was keen to help, there was no chance a sick horse or more horse thieves would enter the barn. And Conan didn't seem the type to kick the wall and hurt himself. He was a happy, confident horse.

She glanced over the rail to where Kat was walking Conan counter clockwise on a loose rein. Nikki had been hoping for a chance to talk, but it was obvious Kat was remaining on the track, staying far away from reporters. And Nikki wanted to drop by Ashley Robart's house and ask a few more questions before the girl left for school.

She walked along the horse path toward her car, excited with what she'd seen. Unless Conan had a complete meltdown, it seemed he'd put on a good show on Saturday. He might not win but he'd make his connections proud.

She stepped back to give a prancing gray gelding lots of room, surprised to see the rider was Sophia. The woman looked comfortable on a horse, but her pinched face showed she wasn't very happy.

"Is he finished his work?" Sophia asked. She didn't say the horse's name but it was obvious she was asking about Conan.

"Yes, the track is still closed but he should be off it soon. Kat is just cooling him out."

"I know that," Sophia snapped. "But Jim insisted I keep an eye on them. Give the horse some company so he doesn't act up and hurt himself. As if I don't have better things to do than babysit Rachel's horse."

Sophia was still muttering as she continued along the horse path, but her words were lost in the wind, and Nikki doubted it was anything complimentary.

She and Gunner both sped up. Soon Conan would be stabled at Santa Anita, far away from all the undercurrents and bruised feelings. He'd be safe there, with time to settle in before the Derby. Justin's trainer had agreed to provide a stall, perhaps a little reluctantly considering Wellington's influence. But Justin had been insistent.

Best of all, Rachel would no longer have to depend on favors from her ex-husband. All in all, things were looking up. But as Nikki drove away, she couldn't quiet her prick of apprehension. Because it was still five days before the race.

And a lot could happen in five days.

CHAPTER SIXTEEN

Kat sat deep in the saddle, letting Conan settle into their cooling-out routine. Her legs still trembled from the workout. Not from fear, never from fear with him, but from the pure thrill of feeling such power. He'd been perfect this morning, hitting every split exactly as planned. The only negative note was that Jim had been watching from his van, parked right by the rail as if trying to make her aware of his presence.

The thought of him soured her mood. Lately he'd been hanging around the barn, finding excuses to talk to her mom. Trying to make himself indispensable. She'd caught him watching her on the track too, his wheelchair positioned where he could see everything. Just like the old days when he used to watch all the young riders.

She pushed the memories away, determined to focus instead on Conan's even stride. He felt so sound, so tough. His neck was low and relaxed as they walked along the backstretch rail. Birds trilled from nearby trees, a much more peaceful serenade than the usual barn chatter.

These quiet moments were what she loved most, just her and Conan. As soon as she returned to the barn, she'd call his jockey with a full report. Elena would be thrilled to hear that he was physically and mentally ready. All their careful preparation was paying off. Even her mom was smiling, really smiling, for the first time in months.

Hoof beats sounded from behind, stealing away the serenity. Kat glanced over her shoulder, recognizing Sophia and her gray gelding. She quickly turned her gaze forward, staring over Conan's ears, hoping Sophia would take the hint. But the gelding pulled alongside them, irritatingly close.

"Jim says I have to stay with you," Sophia said. Her helmet sat crooked, clearly protecting an expensive hairstyle rather than her head. "It's been a while since I had to pony a horse."

Kat kept her body loose, trying to remain unbothered by the intrusion. True, horses preferred company, but Conan was exceptionally brave. And she wasn't about to thank Jim for sending his girlfriend, probably just to make Sophia feel important.

It was so obvious what he was doing. Sending Sophia to "help" was just another way to look good in her mother's eyes. "Look how I'm taking care of your horse and daughter, Rachel." The same calculated concern he'd been showing since they'd arrived with Conan. Every gesture seemed designed to impress her mother, to remind her of how attentive he could be. As if any of them needed his assistance.

"Just keep some distance," Kat murmured, noting how the gray pranced. He probably hadn't been ridden for weeks and certainly wasn't a good escort. Not like Sonny who was always calm and reliable. "Last thing we need is for Conan to get kicked."

"I know that," Sophia snapped. "I've been riding here longer than you."

Not much longer, Kat thought. She, Ashley and Sophia had all started galloping horses around the same time. Ashley had shown the most natural talent, fearlessly exploring the mountain trails. The memory of Ashley's confidence, her bright laugh, made the last of Kat's pleasure drain away. Now Ashley never came near horses. Never left her house. All because of Jim.

"Though luckily we won't have to put up with each other much longer." Sophia's smug voice interrupted Kat's brooding thoughts. "Jim's selling the property. We're moving to Australia as soon as the deal closes."

Kat's head whipped around, shock overriding her determination to stay silent. "Australia?"

"Yes, fresh start. New life together." Sophia's smile held triumph. "Away from all this unpleasantness."

Despite herself, Kat felt a hint of respect for Sophia's dedication. Some women would run from a relationship with a man confined to a wheelchair. But Sophia seemed committed to building a life with Jim, even if it meant leaving everything else behind. If only she knew the truth.

"You'd leave California for him?" Kat couldn't stop her lip from curling in revulsion, though it wasn't about the wheelchair. "Your horse, friends, family?"

"Jim's all I want." Sophia's voice turned dreamy. "You'll understand when you're older. When you find someone who really loves you."

Kat bit back what she knew about Jim Turner's capacity for love. About the way he groomed innocent girls. About Ashley's horrified face that last morning. Instead she asked, "When do you leave?"

"As soon as the property sells. Jim says with his settlement coming, we can—"

A sharp crack split the morning peace. White rail splintered inches from Conan's head. He leaped sideways, colliding with Sophia's gray, his powerful shoulder sending the smaller horse staggering. Kat's hands moved automatically, pulling Conan in a tight circle as instinct took over. Sophia fought to regain control, yanking her reins as she shifted in the saddle.

Another crack echoed and Sophia toppled from the saddle. Her horse wheeled, galloping in a panic toward the gap, but Kat barely noticed. She shortened the reins, staring in horror at Sophia's body, the crimson stain on her blond hair...her unseeing eyes.

Clarity struck with stunning force. Someone was shooting at Conan but had hit Sophia. Without conscious thought, she urged him toward the broken rail, still down after Sonny's misadventure. Conan sailed over the tilted rail, his stride eating up the ground as they tore along the road.

"Go, go, go!" she yelled, her body low over his neck. Every second they were exposed was another chance for the shooter. Her heart hammered as she listened for the rifle. Would she even hear the next shot? She vaguely remembered something from science class about bullets traveling faster than sound. You'd be dead before you heard the crack.

She pressed Conan for even more speed as they thundered across the trailhead parking lot. Every lengthening stride carried them farther away, but was it enough? What range did a rifle have? She'd seen the splintered rail, saw how the bullet had ripped into Sophia's skull.

Endless moments later they were galloping through sheltering trees. She sawed at the reins, now desperate to slow his reckless flight. A branch nearly knocked her from the saddle, but she clung to his mane and yanked him onto a steeper path, using the incline to force him to slow.

Her breath came in ragged gasps. Someone had just shot Sophia. And they'd been aiming for Conan. Were those Saudi men back? Or was it someone else? Questions spiraled through her mind, but survival instinct took over. She guided Conan deeper into the woods, where shadows offered concealment and multiple trails might confuse the gunman.

Theories had to wait. Right now she needed to focus on one thing: keeping them both alive.

CHAPTER SEVENTEEN

Hoof beats echoed against packed dirt as Conan climbed steadily upward, putting distance between them and the track. But Kat's skin prickled with the wary sense of the hunted.

Every few strides, she twisted in the saddle, scanning for movement, imagining armed men behind every tree. Sunlight filtered through branches, creating shifting patterns that made her flinch. When a hawk's cry pierced the quiet, she jerked on the reins before recognizing the familiar sound.

Conan's ears flicked back, accepting her mistake. She stroked him in apology, his neck sweaty beneath her palm. However he moved confidently, as if this rough trail was just another training exercise. His confidence made her racing pulse feel all the more frantic.

In the valley below, the pale oval of the track was still visible. She searched desperately for movement, for any sign of emergency vehicles, but the distance left everything blurred. The horror of what she'd witnessed kept replaying in her mind—the crack of gunfire, the splintering wood, the thud of Sophia's body.

She felt lost, directionless. Her phone sat useless, back in the barn, banned from the track by both facility rules and her mother's insistence. Now that rule, meant to keep riders focused, left her cut off from help.

The trail lay ahead, empty of hikers. The ground turned even more treacherous, loose stones shifting beneath his increasingly shorter steps. Even the usual morning birdsong had fallen silent, as if the forest itself sensed danger. When his hooves struck rock, Kat winced. One stone bruise now would destroy their Derby dreams.

She pulled him to a halt, fear warring with the need to protect his feet. His aluminum racing plates offered little protection against rock. They were designed for manicured dirt tracks, not this rugged terrain.

Every instinct screamed at her to keep moving, to put more distance between Conan and whoever had shot Sophia, but she couldn't risk injuring him. Saturday's Derby represented her mother's life work, the culmination of years of sacrifice and struggle. Her mom had mortgaged everything for this horse, and would likely never have another of Conan's talent.

The rocky trail appeared to twist back to Mountain View. Following it might let her see what was happening at the barn, but one wrong step would send them plunging into the canyon. Another narrow path branched east, its surface more dirt than stone. Low-hanging branches would make it tough for a rider, but at least the footing would be kinder to Conan's feet.

She slapped at a persistent horse fly, weighing her options. The main trail behind them stretched empty, morning mist long burned away. The rocky trail would hide Conan's tracks but might damage his feet. The eastward path looked softer but was dangerously narrow. A wrong choice now could be disastrous.

She glanced back, relieved to see they'd left no obvious sign. However, either of these trails could hide a shooter. But if it was the Saudis hunting Conan, they'd likely stick to the main path.

They didn't know these mountains and might expect her to take the most direct route down.

She urged Conan eastward, away from the center. His stride lengthened on the softer ground. A rabbit darted in front of him but he didn't spook, just watched it with pricked ears.

His calm acceptance of new environments would serve him well at Santa Anita. He'd learned to trust his handlers. Some Derby contenders fell apart in the paddock, overwhelmed by the crowds and noise. Conan's ability to accept surprises might prove as valuable as his speed.

This was actually valuable training, she told herself. And the dirt trail wasn't too narrow. It wound between brush and old oaks, their branches creating shadows that protected him from the sun. Perfect for a horse. Perfect for an ambush.

She pushed away those crippling thoughts. Dwelling on the danger wouldn't help either of them. Better to absorb some of Conan's courage. However, that was easier said than done. And when a covey of quail burst from the brush, wings whirring in flight, she jumped while Conan only flicked an ear. Kat silently scolded herself. If a supposedly flighty Thoroughbred could remain composed through gunfire and mountain trails, surely she could find the same courage.

She squared her shoulders then seconds later had to duck beneath a low-hanging branch as the trail corkscrewed downward. Within minutes, she'd lost her sense of direction.

Ashley would have known exactly where this winding path led. Her friend had spent hours exploring these trails on Sonny, finding hidden meadows and secret routes. No one knew the trails better, except Jim. And after what happened last October, neither Jim nor Ashley had ever ridden again.

Sophia would never ride again either, Kat thought then shoved away her grief, knowing she had to concentrate if she were to save Conan. Though in truth, he had taken over their escape, picking his way over fallen trees, refusing to let any obstacle stop him. A red-tailed hawk circled overhead, its cry echoing off granite walls. She ducked lower over Conan's neck, though the rational part of her mind knew the hawk wasn't what she should fear.

A sound caught her ear, something out of place in the woods. She eased Conan to a stop, trying to listen. Wildlife? Or was someone following? Could be Wellington's people. They could ride, though she doubted they'd murder a horse. But right now, she wasn't prepared to trust her judgment.

She loosened her reins and Conan continued shouldering his way through the trees, branches scraping her skin. She had no idea how long they'd been out here, but he'd need water soon. Surely by now, her mom would have mounted a search. But others would be looking too. And the killer had a head start.

The sun climbed higher while sweat darkened Conan's neck, extending back to his flanks and attracting scores of deer flies. She swiped at them, desperate to find water. He'd need to graze as well. She couldn't let him lose condition before the big race, or worse, risk a bout of colic. But the dense tree cover made it impossible to see ahead, impossible to know which direction might lead to a stream.

A sob caught in her throat as Conan swerved, bulldozing through thick brush and letting branches whip her face. She flattened herself along his neck, unable to do anything else but give him her trust. Then she heard it, water trickling somewhere below, barely audible above the rising wind. Ashley had showed her pictures of a hidden meadow, spring-fed and sheltered by towering pines. And Conan seemed determined to find it.

She gasped as he cut down an impossibly steep bank, almost sliding on his haunches. His focus was absolute, targeting something. And she was merely along for the ride. If it was the meadow, they'd have water and grazing, a good place to keep him quiet while they waited for rescue.

Surely her mom would be mounted by now, hopefully on dependable Sonny. He and Conan were friends, and horses could track each other by scent as well as any dog. Conan was certainly proving that now, nose lifted as he followed the smell of water.

He picked up his trot, twisting between two trees, forcing her to flatten against his back to avoid a low branch. When she straightened, the brown tree trunks had given way to a vibrant green, with a spring bubbling through moss-covered stones.

"You wonderful horse," she said, stroking his neck while he drank deeply from the spring. The psychic had stressed that Conan needed constant praise and recognition. Yet for the last several hours she'd been focused on escaping, had forgotten that need. But he'd been magnificent: accepting strange trails, ignoring wildlife and somehow finding this refuge.

He'd grown up, she thought, lifting a rein and turning him away from the water, knowing he'd had enough for now. She dismounted, feeling exposed on the ground but accepting she had to give his back a rest. She was light, but her mother always stressed that horses weren't machines and hadn't been built to carry a rider.

After loosening the girth, she unknotted her reins to make a lead line. Considered removing the bit so he could chew better, but didn't want to risk losing control.

She tried focusing on his peaceful grazing, the steady rhythm of his teeth tearing grass and how his silky tail swished away the flies. The meadow was a brilliant find. She could spot anyone approaching on the lower trail. And the thick brush around them offered several escape routes, though she hated the thought of pushing Conan through that tangle.

But she couldn't relax. Every rustle and snapping twig made her heart kick. A distant siren wailed, but she had no idea of its location. Sounds carried strangely in these mountains.

She removed her helmet and rubbed her sweaty forehead, trying to make sense of the morning's violence. She kept picturing Sophia's bloody head, the way the bullet had knocked her from the saddle. It had to have been someone on the other side of the track. A bunch of cars had been parked by the grandstand, but she'd assumed they belonged to media. The shooter could have been anyone.

The Saudis seemed obvious suspects. They'd threatened Conan directly, even showed up armed. But would they risk murder just to keep him from racing? Wellington had more reason to want Conan gone. Both his reputation and training operation would take a hit if Conan proved him wrong. But her mom insisted he was a horseman who loved the industry. It seemed crazy that he'd resort to such desperate measures.

Conan's head shot up, ears pricked toward the lower trail. Kat held her breath, listening. Maybe a hiker—someone with a phone she could borrow. If there was no coverage here, she could ask them to make an emergency call at the trailhead.

But silence returned and Conan resumed grazing. She didn't know whether to feel relieved or disappointed. Until she knew what was out there, staying hidden seemed the best option.

CHAPTER EIGHTEEN

Nikki paused in front of Ashley Robart's front door, torn about disturbing the family again. But when she rang the bell, Ashley herself answered. Her baggy sweats were the same, but something had shifted in her expression. A bit less haunted, more determined. She stepped outside, holding Nikki's gaze, her eyes clear and steady instead of darting away as they had during their first meeting.

"I wondered when you'd come back," Ashley said, closing the door behind her. "After what the psychic said about Conan, you probably figured out that the accident wasn't his fault."

Nikki blinked, caught off guard. "You know about the psychic?"

"Kat told me. When her mom first brought him to Mountain View." Ashley's mouth lifted in a hint of a smile. "That's when I knew they finally had a good horse. He just needed someone to understand him. Conan wasn't the problem that morning."

"Can you tell me what happened?"

"He was listening to his rider," Ashley said, her voice so low Nikki could barely hear it. "That's all I can say. I just don't want you to think he's dangerous."

Nikki's phone buzzed. Rachel. Something must be wrong. She'd just seen the woman. Rachel wouldn't call so soon without a good reason.

Nikki answered quickly, her mind racing through possibilities. Had Conan come back lame after his workout? A seemingly perfect gallop could mask a brewing issue that only showed up once muscles cooled.

"Sophia's been shot!" Rachel said, her voice cracking with panic. "Over an hour ago. Kat and Conan escaped into the mountains. Someone saw them gallop up the trail. They looked okay but—" A sob broke through. "They won't let us search for them. The police have the whole area locked down."

"Are the trails locked down too?" Nikki caught Ashley's sharp intake of breath. She moved away from the girl and lowered her voice.

"Yes, and they won't let us near the trailhead." Rachel's voice shook. "Rolf was the first one to reach Sophia, but the police won't let him or anyone else follow. They're treating the entire area as a crime scene. No one in or out while they gather evidence."

"So Kat and Conan are out there alone? Is Sophia okay?"

"She's d-dead. They found her on the track. And there's a bullet hole in the rail. Technicians are here now."

"I'm coming back." Nikki's fingers tightened around the phone, her chest constricting as the news about Sophia sank in. A woman she'd just seen—dead. And now Kat and Conan were fleeing in those unfamiliar mountains, possibly being hunted. Her throat went dry at the thought of the teen alone up there, witnessing a murder and then running for her life. "Maybe I can find a way in that's not so close to the property. But we need advice from someone who knows those mountains."

"I'll talk to Jim," Rachel said. "He knows the trails. But he's in shock. He was in his van by the rail, saw two men in dark clothes running between the barns. Didn't realize Sophia was shot until he saw her horse running loose."

Ashley edged closer, trying to listen. Nikki frowned but the girl just gave a stubborn head shake. And truthfully her interest was a good change. "I'll be there in twenty minutes," Nikki said, ending the call and jogging to her car.

"Jim does know those trails," Ashley called, hurrying after her. "But remember he hates Conan. He'd probably be glad if the horse ran off a cliff. He might not be any help."

"Maybe, but we can still ask. He's always eager to help Rachel."

"There's a meadow where Kat might be able to keep Conan safe," Ashley said. "If she can find it."

"Where's the meadow?" Nikki asked, already yanking open her driver's door.

"Up past the second switchback, where the main trail gets rocky. There's a smaller path that branches east and goes down a steep bank." Ashley's words tumbled out with growing confidence. "Spring-fed, lots of grass. You can't see it from the main trail so it's a good place to hide."

Nikki slid behind the wheel, surprised when Ashley grabbed the door, stopping it from closing.

"I don't think you should trust what Jim says about the trails," Ashley said. "Or anything else."

Nikki studied the girl's face. Saw the fear warring with determination. And determination had won.

"Thanks. I'll remember that," she said, nodding in respect at Ashley's courage. She wished she had time to hear what else the girl might reveal, but Kat and Conan needed her. They might not even be together. Kat could be lying hurt somewhere while Conan might keep running until he broke a leg.

Her phone buzzed just as she was pulling out of the subdivision.

"You okay, Nik?" Justin's voice held the tight control she recognized from his homicide scenes, the practiced neutrality that meant he was worried. "Heard there was an active crime scene at Mountain View. Multiple units responding."

"I'm fine. Just heading there now." She accelerated around a slow-moving truck, adrenaline making her driving more aggressive than usual. "One woman is dead, and Kat and Conan are somewhere in the woods. Can you get me in? So Gunner can search?"

"I'll see what I can do. But it's not our jurisdiction." His careful neutrality remained intact, but she guessed he was already working angles, calling in favors. He never held back resources when she needed them, regardless of the professional cost. "Stay safe, Nik. If someone's targeting the facility..."

He let the implications hang, both of them knowing how quickly violence could escalate when suspects felt cornered.

"I know." She swallowed against the tightness in her throat. Even with their respective experiences, neither took risks lightly. And she always worried about Gunner's safety. Too many K9s had been injured on similar operations—falling down ravines, encountering predators, or worse, being deliberately hurt by the people they tracked. "But Kat's out there alone. And someone's already killed once today."

She ended the call and turned onto Mountain View's drive. Yellow crime scene tape stretched across the entrance, fluttering in the breeze. Three patrol cars and an unmarked detective's vehicle blocked the road, their emergency lights spinning. A crime scene van was parked by the grandstand, technicians pulling on gloves and gathering equipment. Through the row of barns, she could see another van on the far side of the track.

She pulled up to the barricade where a uniformed officer conferred with a detective. The officer broke away, approaching her car with measured steps. His hand hovered near his holster, his expression stony.

"Sorry ma'am, active crime scene. No one in or out."

"I'm a licensed PI," Nikki said, showing her credentials. "I installed surveillance cameras a few days ago along this drive. They should catch any vehicles that entered this way."

The detective stepped forward, his eyes narrowed. "Where exactly?"

"Hidden in the bougainvillea. Should give clear shots of license plates."

The men conferred in low voices, the detective's interest clearly sharpened by the thought of footage. After a brief discussion, the officer turned back to her car.

"The detective wants those surveillance files as soon as possible. They'll forward you a download address. Stay by the first barn. The track and trailhead are off limits until we process the scene."

Nikki gave her most sincere nod, already trying to figure out a way around the restrictions. She parked near Rachel's truck, positioning herself where she could see the track. Evidence markers dotted the oval while technicians snapped photos. Rachel stood near the horse path, only thirty feet away, staring bleakly at the treed slope where her daughter had disappeared.

"Hey," Nikki called, conscious of the officer monitoring her movements.

Rachel rushed over, her face tear-stained. "Poor Sophia. It's horrible. Jim's been talking to her parents. Maybe Conan really *is* bad luck."

Nikki remained silent. While Rachel was fixated on Conan as the target, something nagged at her, like a shadow glimpsed from the corner of her eye. Present but not fully formed.

"Kat could be hurt out there," Rachel went on. "She's a good rider but even Olympic riders get thrown. And those mountain trails are treacherous. She and Conan aren't used to that sort of terrain."

"Has anyone checked local emergency rooms? In case hikers found her?"

"The police called them all." Rachel rubbed her bloodshot eyes. "Nothing yet. I'm not even thinking about Conan anymore. If he hurts himself up there and is suffering, I'll do what's best for him. I just want Kat to come home safe."

Nikki paced a circle by the barn, her mind sifting through options. She could try hiking in from the west side of the mountain, but it might take too long for Gunner to get close enough to pick up a scent. And every minute increased the chance of Kat being hurt. She checked her phone again, willing it to buzz with news from Justin.

When it finally did, her heart sank. Justin's text: *Can get you access by end of day. Best I can do.*

That wasn't good enough. She wouldn't be able to start a search in the dark. And tomorrow might be too late. She hit speed dial.

"Sonja? I need your help," she said, updating her friend on the tragedy. "Can you connect with Conan? Find out if he and Kat are okay?"

Sonja was silent for a moment. "That's awful," she finally said. Nikki heard a drawer opening. "Just a sec. I have a file here, his pictures."

The wait seemed endless but Nikki forced herself to stay silent, hoping. When Sonja spoke again, there was humor in her voice. "He's eating. Really likes the grass. And the water has a different taste, a flavor he likes."

"Is Kat with him?"

"I don't know. He's just thinking of grass and water. Seems content."

So for now, Conan was safe, Nikki thought. But was Kat hurt? There was no way she and Gunner would stand back if the girl was lying somewhere. She studied the mountains looming beyond the track. There had to be a way in that avoided the police cordon.

"Wait," Sonja said. A long pause. "His person's with him. Must be Kat. He's being very careful with her. Feeling protective."

Nikki's knees weakened with relief and she gave Rachel a thumbs-up. "Where are they? Can you get a location?"

"He's a horse," Sonja said dryly. "I can only get his feelings, images. But it's a place with grass and water, and he likes it."

"Thank you, Sonja," Nikki said, as Rachel hurried over, visibly relieved. "And Kat's mother thanks you too."

"They're still together," Nikki said, palming her phone and smiling at Rachel. "But they can't stay up there all night. It gets too cold and anything could spook him. Can you ask Jim about other access points? Something outside the police cordon?"

Rachel nodded and pulled out her phone. While she was talking to Jim, Nikki emailed her surveillance footage to the police. Then she returned to her car and checked her pack, mentally ticking off essentials. Extra water, protein bars, dog food for

Gunner. She added a light jacket for Kat and a halter. Her Glock went in last. Those mountains might hold more dangers than just cold and darkness.

Rachel joined her, disappointment evident in the way she gripped her phone. "Jim says it's hopeless. Nearest access is ten miles north then you'd have to bushwhack across a forested ridge. It would take at least ten hours to reach the area."

Something about Jim's too-quick response bothered Nikki. This was the same man who'd quickly cleared the track, secured a trailer for Sonny and assigned Rolf as night guard when needed. Jim Turner was a problem solver—calculating, resourceful, always ready with solutions. His abrupt dismissal without even pausing to consider alternatives seemed strikingly out of character.

Ashley's warning echoed in her mind: "Remember he hates Conan. He'd probably be glad if the horse ran off a cliff." Nikki waited until Rachel was distracted by police then pulled out her phone and called Ashley.

"The next closest access is ten miles away?" Ashley's voice dripped sarcasm. "That's what Jim told you? He's wrong. There's a fire road off Canyon Drive, maybe two miles south. Connects right to the main trail system. I used it all the time."

Nikki found it and quickly entered the coordinates. "Any other advice?" she asked.

"Yeah. Don't tell Jim which trail you're taking. He'd probably tell the police, trying to come off as helpful."

"Thanks." Nikki ended the call, mulling over Ashley's warning. Jim might be happy if Conan didn't return safely, after being paralyzed by the horse. Others might also benefit if Conan had an accident. It would certainly prove Wellington right about the horse, especially after all the negative press.

She punched in Mike Jensen's number, hoping to control some of the inevitable speculation.

"Already writing the story," he answered, keyboard clicks carrying through the line. "My source contacted me right after it happened."

"Pretty quick with those details." She remembered his last suspiciously timed blog post. "Again."

A pause, filled only with the soft hum of his computer. "Yeah, that's been bothering me since our talk yesterday. Almost like they were ready with the story."

"Any chance you'll tell me who it is?"

"You know I can't. But I am rethinking some of their earlier claims." Jensen sighed. "Story would get massive hits. '*Derby Contender Forces Deadly Mountain Chase.*' Readers love this stuff."

"Conan didn't force anything. Someone shot at him. And his rider was smart enough to get away."

"Won't matter now. Even if they find him alive, that horse won't be racing Saturday. Not after running loose in those mountains. But keep me posted. I'd rather write the truth than propaganda. Even if it gets fewer clicks."

She ended the call and turned to Rachel who hovered nearby, worry etched on her face. "I need something with Kat's scent," Nikki said. "A jacket or shirt she's worn recently. And something from Conan."

"Her sweatshirt is in the tack room," Rachel said, wheeling away. "And I'll get Conan's stable wraps. He wore them last night."

She raced back with Kat's sweatshirt and a soiled bandage. Nikki sealed them in separate plastic bags and tucked them in her pack, making sure to keep her Glock on top. The shooter had obviously been aiming for Conan. Tragically Sophia had been in the wrong place. But Kat was up there too, alone and vulnerable after witnessing a murder. She might be in danger now, more than the horse.

The mountains dominated the horizon, far too much territory to search without a plan. Even if Kat had stayed on, a frightened Thoroughbred would be tough to control. But there was no time to wait for search and rescue teams, or police permission. Somewhere up there, a killer might also be hunting. And she had to find them first, before he decided Kat was just as expendable as Sophia.

CHAPTER NINETEEN

The fire road looked more like an overgrown game trail, barely visible between thick bushes. Without Ashley's directions, Nikki would have missed the sagging wooden post marking public access.

She parked on the side of the road. Scorching air blasted her face when she opened the door, the contrast with the air conditioning jarring. From here, Mountain View's buildings were invisible, though as the crow flies they weren't more than two miles away. The police cordon might as well have been in another county.

Gunner waited eagerly while she fitted his tracking harness, its reflective strips catching the noon sun. This was his favorite kind of game. She pulled Conan's wrap from its plastic bag, holding it out for him to smell.

"Find," she said, hoping Kat hadn't been thrown. The teen's sweatshirt remained sealed in her pack, a backup plan she prayed wouldn't be needed.

Gunner pressed his nose against the cotton wrap, processing the scent before wheeling toward the path. Nikki hurried after him, her pack settling against her shoulders. The breeze stirred pine needles overhead, carrying hints of sage and dusty earth. Bird calls echoed through the canyon, their peaceful sounds mocking her urgency. Each passing minute increased the chances of Kat and

Conan being lost or hurt. She wasn't sure which would be worse, given who else might be searching.

She tried not to think about the third possibility: that they might already be beyond help.

The path twisted through oak and pine, forcing them to climb in sharp turns. A western tanager flashed orange through branches, its melodic call echoing between the trees. In other circumstances, this would be a pleasant hike. But the bird's cheerful song and brilliant plumage was out of place against the backdrop of their desperate search.

Sweat trickled down her back as they climbed. The fire road narrowed into a dirt trail, crossing other paths that branched in three directions. A young couple with daypacks passed them, heading down.

"Beautiful day for a hike," the woman called.

"Have you seen any horses up there? Maybe a loose one? Saddled?"

They shook their heads. "Just some deer. And lots of squirrels."

Gunner kept casting around, but his lack of excitement suggested they weren't on the right trail yet. They passed through a stand of massive pines, their shade offering brief relief from the heat. When they emerged, a hawk wheeled overhead, riding thermals in lazy circles against the blue sky, searching methodically for any movement that might signal prey. Nikki watched its efficient pattern with wistful admiration. She should have brought her drone. It would cover ten times the ground in half the time. She made a mental note to keep it in her car from now on, alongside her other emergency gear.

Just beyond the pines, where the trail turned east, fresh hoof prints marked the ground. She crouched, studying the impressions.

Two sets were deeply pressed into the dirt, indicating substantial weight, at least a thousand pounds. But these weren't the marks left by racing plates. The indentations showed the broader, heavier pattern of recreational trail horses with standard steel shoes.

Conan didn't make these tracks. However horses were a herd animal and he might have sought other horses, especially if he was frightened. Despite Gunner's reluctance, she called him to heel and followed the prints for the next half mile. A small camp appeared through the trees, an older couple by their tent, two hobbled Appaloosas grazing nearby.

"Looking for someone?" the man asked, noting her disappointment.

She explained briefly about Kat and Conan.

"Haven't seen them. But there are dozens of trails up here. Horse could be anywhere. Might have joined some wild ones."

"Need a break?" the woman offered, gesturing toward their camping chairs. "We've got coffee. Or cold drinks in the cooler."

"Thanks, but I need to keep moving." She'd wasted precious minutes following these prints, letting human logic override Gunner's training. A mistake that had cost them valuable time.

She retraced their steps to the main trail, pausing in a patch of shade to take several deep swigs of water and to fill Gunner's collapsible bowl. But they didn't linger. Those wasted minutes gnawed at her.

Time to change tactics. She pulled out Kat's sweatshirt. A panicked horse might run anywhere, but Kat would move much slower. If she was on foot or hurt, she'd be closer to the center. And if she'd somehow kept her seat on Conan, she'd make strategic choices—seeking water, grass, somewhere safe. Kat galloped racehorses: She knew how to think under pressure.

Gunner's nose worked over the sweatshirt. "Find," Nikki said, relieved to see him moving with fresh purpose, nose testing the wind. A deer bounded across their path, white tail flashing, but he stayed focused. Not even a darting rabbit broke his concentration.

He led her eastward on a game trail that left her crawling beneath several downed trees. Slow going, but she trusted her partner. The air cooled as they climbed, the sun slanting toward the west. Her legs burned and her pack felt twice as heavy, but Gunner showed no sign of fatigue. If anything, his pace quickened.

He stopped, head high, nose lifted in the breeze. His body tensed with that familiar alertness that indicated a strong scent. He surged forward, leading her along a narrow trail bordering a steep drop. The path wound between granite boulders, the huge rocks still warm from the sun.

Though the main trail had been well traveled, this one showed little use. Perfect for someone trying to stay hidden. She half ran, half slid down the steep bank, loose stones skittering beneath her boots as she followed Gunner into a grassy meadow. A spring trickled over mossy rocks, and hoof prints marked the damp earth where a horse had recently drank.

Her heart leaped. The manure was fresh and the grass showed signs of recent grazing as well as flattened patches where a horse had stood. But there was no sign of Conan. And the sun had dropped, painting the sky in shades of amber. If she didn't find them soon, they'd all face a dangerous night in these mountains.

But Gunner circled the meadow, undaunted, then twisted and led her into the trees. A large shape materialized in the gathering dusk. Conan stood in a small clearing, watching their approach. Kat sat cross-legged on the ground, her back pressed against a fallen log. Gunner charged forward, his tail sweeping in excited circles. Then he sat, his signal for a successful find.

"Gunner!" Kat's face lit up. She wrapped her arms around him in an enthusiastic hug before scrambling to her feet, dried leaves clinging to her riding pants. When she noticed Nikki, her grin turned to pure relief.

"I can't believe you found us." Then reality crashed back and her smile vanished. "Sophia? She's dead, isn't she?"

Nikki gave a regretful nod, watching the girl's face tighten with sorrow.

"Do they know who did it? Why didn't anyone come sooner?" Kat's words tumbled out, grief giving way to questions. "Is Mom okay?"

"She's frantic about you," Nikki said, tossing Gunner his reward ball. "But the police have the whole area locked down. Won't let anyone in or out while they investigate."

"But you're here. And Gunner."

"Ashley told us about another access point." She touched Kat's shoulder, feeling the slight tremor that belied the girl's composure. "Are you hurt?"

Kat shook her head. "No, but we're so tired of hiding."

Nikki studied them both with growing amazement. Kat's clothes were dusty and torn from branches, but aside from shallow scratches on her face and arms, she seemed unharmed. And Conan—the supposedly high-strung racehorse—stood quietly. His neck and back were marked with dried sweat but his eyes were bright. They'd handled the crisis with amazing poise.

"You did an incredible job looking after him," Nikki said.

"It was more him looking after me," Kat admitted, reaching up to stroke Conan's neck. "I was terrified. Wasn't thinking straight, not at first. But we couldn't run forever. And he made it easy to hide." Pride crept into her voice. "Like he understood what we needed to do."

"We need to get you both back. It'll be dark soon. Luckily we're not too far from the center. There looks like a decent trail down—"

Gunner's sudden growl cut through the quiet, his hackles lifting as he stared into the trees.

Kat sucked in a breath, her voice lowering. "I think someone's looking for us. And Conan keeps staring in that direction. It's weird. They never call my name. If it was search and rescue, wouldn't they be shouting? Whoever it is seems to be sneaking around. That's why we left the meadow and hid."

Nikki noted Gunner's rigid stance, then glanced at Conan, whose ears were fixed on the same wooden section. People often imagined threats, especially as shadows lengthened and nerves frayed. But animals were rarely wrong.

Her dog's growl and raised hackles weren't his alert to deer or rabbits—this was a serious threat. Someone was moving through those trees. Someone patient enough to track Kat this far, skilled enough to stay hidden.

And after what had happened to Sophia, they knew exactly how dangerous that person could be.

CHAPTER TWENTY

Nikki checked her phone. No signal bars. She'd expected as much. These mountains blocked most transmissions, turning the area into a dead zone. She slipped off her pack and pulled out the halter, Kat's sweatshirt and the jacket.

"You must be freezing," she whispered, conscious of their hidden watcher. "Take this stuff. There are protein bars in the pockets."

Kat gratefully tugged on the warm layers then tore open a protein bar. The pallor around her scratches was visible now, adrenaline finally draining away.

"Thanks," she mumbled, her mouth full of nuts and chocolate. "You thought of everything."

Not quite. Nikki wished she'd packed night vision goggles. That would give her the option of going after whoever was in the trees, while staying between him and Kat. But as it stood now, the safest plan required separating.

"Where's your saddle?" she asked.

"Back by the spring." Kat's voice barely carried. "I took it off so Conan could roll and get comfortable. Didn't think we'd be up here this long."

Nikki's mind raced as Kat devoured a second protein bar. At least the girl was getting calories. She'd need fuel for what lay ahead. But she also needed her saddle. Riding bareback might work on flat ground in daylight, but these trails would be even more treacherous in the dark.

Gunner's head turned slightly, a subtle shift that spoke volumes. Their stalker was moving. Nikki pulled out her Glock and stuck it in the back of her jeans. Their searcher was about thirty yards away, using the thick brush for cover. Patient, unhurried, as if confident he'd eventually find them. And she needed to act now, before he pinpointed their location.

"Stay," she whispered, using the hand signal that both Kat and Gunner understood.

"Are you leaving us?" Kat's voice cracked around a mouthful of bar.

"Just to get your saddle. You'll need it." Nikki kept her voice steady despite her hammering heart. "Gunner will protect you. Don't move from this spot." She pressed the water bottle into Kat's cold hand. "Eat another bar, drink some water. Get ready for a night ride."

Then she edged around the far side of the meadow, using the trees for cover. The spring wasn't far. But in the gathering darkness, every shadow seemed to breathe with menace.

Pine needles muffled her steps and the spring's trickle guided her forward, its steady sound helping mask her movement. Each tree became a tactical choice, offering cover while she listened for anything out of place. The saddle should be just ahead. She'd retrieve it and be back to Kat within minutes.

Moonlight filtered through branches. Seconds later, she caught the glint of light reflecting off steel stirrups. The saddle lay beneath a low-hanging pine, positioned with care to protect the leather. Even in crisis, Kat had wanted to take care of her tack.

Nikki stilled, scanning the trees. No human sounds disturbed the forest's rhythm. Just the whisper of wind and the spring's steady gurgle. She eased forward, scooped up the saddle then pressed against the nearest tree trunk.

The saddle felt reassuring against her chest, but it also left her more vulnerable. Harder to reach her weapon, slower to move, every step requiring a balance between speed and stealth. She couldn't risk noise. Their tracker didn't know Conan's exact location, and she needed to keep that advantage.

An owl's cry pierced the quiet. Her heart jumped before her mind processed the sound. But that cry might have masked other movements. The knowledge pushed her faster, and she sighed with relief when she spotted Conan's dark shape.

"We have to hurry," she breathed, helping Kat slip the saddle onto Conan's warm back. The big horse stood motionless, as if understanding their need for silence. Her throat tightened with gratitude at his cooperation. Most Thoroughbreds in training would be dancing in place, unable to contain their energy.

Racehorses were bred for reactivity, their bodies fueled by high-protein diets designed to build explosive speed. As flight animals, they were hardwired to spook at unfamiliar sounds and movements, especially in threatening environments. Yet Conan remained patiently still, only his ears flicking.

"I don't want to leave you." Kat's voice trembled, her fingers fumbling with the buckle before she was able to tighten the girth.

"It's the best way." Nikki pressed her phone into Kat's palm. "Ride downhill, west, until you get service. Then call for help." She gestured toward the darker trees. "There are low branches but the footing is good. Mostly dirt paths, not much rock."

"Dirt path, that's good. Better for his feet."

The girl's priorities made Nikki smile. Even now, with a killer in the darkness, she was thinking about Conan, trying to conserve him for Saturday's race. Some goals were too deeply ingrained to shake.

"Mount up," Nikki whispered. "Ride out as quiet as you can."

Kat nodded and Nikki legged her into the saddle. Conan shifted slightly and Nikki touched his neck, steadying him. "Horses see better than us at night," she whispered. "Trust him to find the trail. Just keep heading down. You'll come out near my car."

"What about you?" Kat's voice quavered despite her attempt at bravery.

"I'll go the other way, toward Mountain View." She gave Kat's knee a reassuring squeeze. "In a little while, you'll hear gunshots. Don't worry. I'm hoping the police will hear too. Now go."

She watched Conan pick his way between trees, his stride lengthening when he found the trail. Once his shadow disappeared, she turned away. Time to play decoy.

She deliberately let branches rustle, trying to sound like someone leading a big horse, someone attempting stealth but not quite managing. Gunner's low growl confirmed their plan was working. Whoever was searching was following her now, instead of Conan.

She angled uphill, away from Kat's escape route. The ground turned steeper, more treacherous. Each step had to be precise. A turned ankle could be disastrous.

A stone clattered behind them. Close, too close. Gunner twisted, coiled to attack. But she urged him on, deliberately snapping another branch, determined to keep their pursuer focused on them and not listening for distant hoof beats.

The moon slipped behind clouds, plunging the slope into darkness. She eased her way forward, one hand gripping Gunner's harness, the other hovering near her weapon.

They were being hunted now. But that was exactly what she'd planned.

CHAPTER TWENTY-ONE

Nikki's lungs burned as she climbed, one hand on Gunner's shoulders for guidance, the other ready to catch herself if she slipped. Somewhere below, Mountain View's lights should soon be visible, if she could just find enough elevation. But the forest pressed close, brush reaching like gnarled fingers to snag her clothes, the mountain itself seeming to mock her progress.

Gunner's hackles hadn't lowered since they'd started this game of cat and mouse. His subtle shifts told her their pursuer was keeping steady pace, moving almost parallel. The killer seemed to know these trails. Every time she thought she'd gained ground, another snapping branch would signal his presence.

She cupped her watch, shielding the luminous dial. 9:42. Kat had been gone thirty minutes. Not quite long enough. Nikki wanted to give her more time before firing her Glock. The shots would bring rescue, but they'd also pinpoint her location. And she couldn't risk her pursuer figuring out she was alone, then doubling back to chase Kat.

A stone clattered down the slope behind them, closer than before. She pressed against a massive boulder, forcing her breathing to steady. The long-range rifle that had killed Sophia would be lethal if she gave him a clear shot. It only took one mistake, one moment of exposure.

Gunner's head turned, tracking something she couldn't detect. She touched his head, grateful for his keen nose and protective instincts. Without him, she'd have lost their pursuer's position long ago. And every minute they kept moving gave Kat a better chance of reaching help.

"Let's go," she whispered. Gunner's nose lifted, testing the wind before he guided her sharply left. By now, she'd lost all sense of direction. Her legs burned with fatigue, lungs straining in the thin air. It couldn't be fun for their pursuer either. But maybe he enjoyed the hunt. Relished seeing them as prey.

Her jaw clenched as realization hit. He *was* enjoying this. The hunter stalking his prey through darkness—not opportunism but calculated pursuit. Their stalker moved with purpose, anticipating this tiring climb. Whoever followed them seemed to know exactly where they'd end, as if herding them toward some predetermined spot.

But her fatigue was becoming dangerous. She stumbled over a root and barely caught herself. And Gunner was panting. They couldn't keep climbing forever. The ridge had to be close.

She needed to see Mountain View's lights. But reaching open ground would also mean exposure. They'd be silhouetted against the sky, easy targets. And Gunner's mounting tension told her their pursuer was closing the gap. He'd conserved his energy following a trail while they'd exhausted themselves in rough terrain.

She touched her Glock, comforted by its presence. Kat must have reached the lower trails by now and found cell service. Maybe it was time to risk the shots, bring the search parties. But in that critical time between her gunfire and police response, the killer would have every advantage. And Mountain View's lights remained stubbornly hidden.

A rock tumbled down the slope, followed by the metallic sound of a rifle bolt being worked. The sharp click echoed through the darkness, flooding her with adrenaline. Their pursuer was finished playing.

She crouched behind a fallen log, its rough bark pressing into her ribs. The ridge loomed above, a deadly open space. Below, the slope fell away, too steep to descend. Time to make a stand. But first, she'd choose her ground.

The ridge line was visible through breaks in the stunted trees, showing several granite boulders. Perfect cover, offering several good shooting positions. If she could only reach them.

She hurried toward the boulders, one hand on Gunner's shoulders while the other gripped her Glock. Every sound seemed amplified—her ragged breathing, Gunner's panting, pebbles clicking beneath their feet.

Stones clattered, only twenty feet away. Had to be their pursuer. He moved boldly now, no longer masking his approach, knowing he had her trapped between the ridge and the cliff.

This relentless stalking made no sense. He had to know by now that Conan and Kat were gone. Was he chasing her and Gunner out of vindictiveness? The Saudis weren't the type for personal vengeance. They'd want Conan, not revenge against a private investigator. And cold-blooded murder seemed way beyond Wellington's single minded ambition. Yet their pursuer was enjoying the chase, content to make her sweat. And she'd had enough.

She slipped between two boulders, her mind still sharp despite her exhausted body. She and Justin had practiced this scenario: Gunner was her advantage. He'd tell her exactly where the shooter was.

She watched for Gunner's cues, shifting as he peered left, ears pinned downward. She could hear the man's labored breathing, the scrape of his boots on stone. The moon chose that moment to emerge, throwing harsh light across the exposed ridge. The sudden illumination made the shadows between the boulders seem blacker.

She pressed deeper into those shadows, using the boulders' bulk for cover. The killer would have to step into that revealing moonlight to get a clear shot at her position. Unless... Her heart rate spiked as she realized that might be exactly what he wanted her to think.

Gunner's head snapped toward the right, confirming her fear. The killer wasn't seeking high ground. He was circling to the open end of the boulders, using the same shadows she'd thought would protect them. Like someone who'd hunted this ridge before.

She pulled Gunner close, positioning her body between him and the approaching rifle. She wouldn't let him be the first target—not her partner who only wanted to protect. And her fear hardened into determination. Their pursuer was a bully and a killer, expecting to find a frightened woman and her dog, helpless against a powerful rifle. But they weren't helpless. And if he came for them, she wouldn't hesitate to make a kill shot.

But first: She raised the Glock, steadying her grip with both hands, and fired three rapid shots skyward. The sound crashed against granite walls, the reports thundering through the valley. Each shot multiplied as it bounced between ridge lines, surely carrying down to Mountain View.

Then she shifted position, pulling Gunner with her and dropping into a shooter's stance. Rocks rolled. Branches snapped. It took several seconds for her brain to process what the sounds were saying.

Their pursuer wasn't advancing. He was retreating, crashing through brush, all stealth forgotten. She gulped, scarcely believing what was happening—he hadn't known she was armed. And now he was running like a scared rabbit, unwilling to get in a shootout, bolting away before help could arrive.

"Coward!" she called, her voice carrying both relief and triumph. Her shots had accomplished exactly what she'd hoped. Their hunter had become the hunted.

And he didn't like it.

CHAPTER TWENTY-TWO

"The gunshots helped establish your location." The detective balanced his notebook on the police car's hood, his flashlight casting harsh shadows over his face. "It was fortunate you had your weapon."

Nikki sat on the bumper, legs still aching from the steep mountain descent. Every muscle screamed from the long day. Even Gunner's usual alertness was blunted by exhaustion. She trailed her fingers over his neck, pulling out the sticks and burrs.

"No sign of whoever was chasing us?" Her voice came out rough, sandpaper-dry despite the water bottle she'd just drained.

"Not yet. Terrain's too rough for a night search." He clicked his pen, the sound jarring in the quiet. "We'll get a tracking team up there at first light. You said you caught a glimpse of a rifle?"

"Yes. I assumed it was the murder weapon from this morning." She watched his pen scratch across his notebook, recording details that already seemed distant. Just two hours ago, officers had met her and Gunner on the mountain, rifles ready, powerful flashlights cutting through the dark. Their escort down the steep trail had been efficient but tense, everyone scanning the shadows for movement.

"Has Kat given her statement yet?" she asked.

"No. She's still about two miles out, waiting with her mother and a couple officers. Refuses to leave until the stock trailer arrives."

A smile momentarily softened his face."Says her horse won't load for strangers. Even ones with badges."

She's probably right, Nikki thought. Conan was remarkably obliging with his trusted handlers, but that cooperation likely wouldn't extend to strangers trying to rush him onto an unfamiliar trailer.

She pulled kibble from her pack, offering it to Gunner in her cupped hand. No reason for her partner to wait any longer for his supper. He'd earned it. Without him this night could have ended differently.

"We might have more questions later," the detective said, closing his notebook with a decisive snap. "There's pizza and doughnuts inside. Mr. Turner's been very cooperative. Made his office available. His security guard keeps the coffee fresh. You and your K9 are welcome to wait there while I send someone for your vehicle."

"Thanks, but I'll wait in the barn." She handed him her car keys with a strained smile. The last place she wanted to be was in Jim Turner's office, watching his dogged helpfulness, his determination to please Rachel. And conversely be less than helpful in finding Conan.

The detective's radio crackled as another patrol car cruised along the drive, and he stepped away to receive an update. Crime scene techs were still processing evidence, their floodlights turning night into artificial day. She felt isolated without her phone, still with Kat, and couldn't shake the feeling that nothing about this day made sense.

She rose and walked stiffly toward the barn, Gunner padding beside her.

She settled onto a hay bale outside Conan's empty stall while Gunner flopped at her feet with a tired grunt. Coffee would be nice but she didn't want Jim's hospitality. Something felt wrong about his priorities. Most people would be devastated by their girlfriend's murder, too shocked to serve coffee and pizza.

But maybe she was just tired, seeing shadows where none existed. Her phone would be showing after midnight by now, if she had it. Kat would arrive soon though, once Conan was safely loaded. Then she could update Justin so he wouldn't worry. Although he might still be deep in his homicide case, and not even be aware of all that had happened.

The waiting stretched like a taut wire, each minute pulling tighter. Vehicles whipped past the barn entrance. Some leaving, others arriving. Each time she peered out the end door, hoping to see a horse trailer. But it was just more police, more techs, more people examining what felt like all the wrong things.

Sophia was dead. Yet everyone was focused on Conan as the target, even after the killer had chosen to follow Nikki instead of the horse. Sighing, she leaned back against the stall just as a steaming coffee cup appeared above her lap.

"Marco!" She hadn't expected him until morning, thought he was resting at his home. "Should you be here?"

"Doc says I'm fine." He handed her the cup, his face drawn with concern. "Heard what happened. Came to help with Conan when they bring him in. Kat okay?"

"She's great, so gutsy. Wouldn't leave Conan. And he didn't leave her." Nikki wrapped her fingers around the warm mug, watching Marco check the stall. Even groggy from being drugged, his first thought was for the horse. Despite his slow movements, he dumped the water buckets and hay nets, refusing to take chances with anything that might have been tampered with during his absence.

He ran a pitchfork through the bedding, checking for foreign objects, then inspected the small turnout attached to the stall. His suspicious eye missed nothing: latches, salt licks, even the drainage hole. His painstaking inspection spoke of dedication as well as a newfound understanding of the required vigilance.

"The trailer should be here soon," Nikki said. Like her, Marco kept peering toward the barn door.

"Good." He stooped to pat Gunner's head, his weathered face softening. "Thank you both for bringing them back." The smile that lit up his face meant more because it was so rare and offered a glimpse of the man beneath his reserve.

He shuffled back to the stall and added extra to Conan's haynets. "Horse like that, needs his groom, his people," he said. "And Conan deserves to get what he wants. Especially after all this."

She nodded in total agreement and sipped the coffee, grateful for both its warmth and Marco's undemanding presence. In all the chaos and questions, his devotion to the horse felt like the only normal part of this night.

A diesel engine growled in the parking lot, its headlights cutting bright swaths. Nikki hurried to the door, recognizing the local hauler's rig, the same one that had rescued Sonny. Two patrol cars flanked the rig, but parked a careful distance away.

Kat burst from the first patrol car, her voice carrying across the parking lot as she sprinted toward the barn. She threw her arms around Nikki in a fierce hug. "I'm so glad you and Gunner are okay. Thank you for rescuing us."

She dropped to her knees, wrapping her arms around Gunner's thick neck before rising to include Marco in a fervent embrace. "Conan was wonderful," she told him. "Absolutely wonderful!"

She skipped back to the trailer, youth and excitement masking her exhaustion. Conan also looked surprisingly fresh as Rachel led him down the ramp and into the barn. Though morning light and a vet exam might tell a different story.

Marco ran practiced hands over Conan's legs while Rachel hovered nearby, pointing out every scratch and scrape. The two of them checked every inch of his body, speaking their own quiet language of horsemanship. But Rachel's eyes kept returning to Kat and she watched her daughter with the intensity of someone who'd come too close to losing what mattered most.

Nikki's car keys and phone weighed heavy in her pocket. An officer had retrieved her vehicle and Kat had returned the phone. It showed a dozen missed calls, most from Rachel but several from Sonja and Justin. But right now, watching Conan settle in his stall, surrounded by his devoted team, those calls could wait. Her searches didn't always have happy endings. And getting them out of the mountains alive was a victory that needed to be savored.

A uniformed officer appeared in the doorway, his presence shattering the special moment. "Kat Parker? Detective wants to speak with you."

Kat's hand lingered on Conan's shoulder, as if reluctant to break contact. They'd been together for nearly eighteen hours, depending on each other to survive. Her fingers trembled against his dark coat, the only visible sign of what they'd endured. The bond between them had strengthened during those long hours. If they hadn't been a team before, they certainly were now.

"Go ahead," Marco said softly. "I've got him." He was already reaching for a warm bran mash, its ingredients mixed with loving care.

Kat slipped from the stall but stopped by Nikki. "Thanks again," she said. "For finding us. And for making me leave when you did. It wasn't so scary after you took over. And when you led Sophia's killer away..." She shook her head, her eyes holding shadows no teenager should carry. Nikki squeezed her shoulder, feeling the girl lean into the touch, seeking comfort from someone who'd been there.

"You did the hard part," Nikki said. "You and Conan."

"Kat?" The officer shifted impatiently, duty warring with sensitivity.

"Coming." Kat gave Gunner a final pat before striding toward the officer. Rachel followed closely, radiating the energy of a protective mother grizzly.

But after staring down fear, navigating the mountain and keeping her beloved horse safe, a police interview seemed almost trivial. Kat looked ready to face any sort of interrogation—be it police or media. She moved with a new confidence, the kind that comes from facing the worst and finding yourself equal to the challenge.

However as Nikki watched them go, a hollow feeling replaced her admiration. Everyone assumed the killer was after Conan. That Sophia's death had been the result of a missed shot. Yet their pursuer in the mountains hadn't shown the slightest interest in finding a horse.

He'd been hunting humans.

CHAPTER TWENTY-THREE

A familiar stride echoed through the barn aisle, boot heels striking the floor with measured confidence. The rhythm was unmistakable, purposeful without being rushed, the sound of someone who moved with natural authority. Nikki glanced up from her seat on the hay bale and spotted Justin. Relief flooded through her. She didn't know how he'd driven here so fast, or how he'd known to come, but he seemed to have a sixth sense about when she needed him, even if she'd never admit that she did.

"Hey, Nik," he said, crouching to examine the scratches on her face. Gunner circled eagerly, demanding his share of attention. Justin obliged, his knowing hands moving over the dog's body and legs, checking for any injuries that might have been missed. Satisfied that Gunner was unharmed, he straightened and pulled Nikki to her feet, holding her tighter than usual.

"Didn't think you'd feel like driving home tonight," he murmured.

"I'm fine, just catching my breath before getting in my car. I could always sleep in the barn for a bit." Even to her ears, the words sounded unconvincing.

"Heard you spent most of the day in a search and rescue op, then had to evade a killer. You'll sleep better at home not worrying about the horse. So will Gunner." His tone was gentle but firm. "We can pick up your car later."

Marco stepped out of Conan's stall, nodding at Nikki. "I'm watching Conan. And there are police everywhere. He's extra safe tonight."

Justin looked over the stall door where Conan's nose was buried in his bran mash, enthusiastically licking his feed tub. "He looks great, considering everything. Hard to believe this is Wellington's renegade."

"I've come to accept he's no outlaw," Nikki said. "Thought he'd panic and run off a cliff. But he has an exceptional mind."

"Lieutenant Decker!" They all turned as the detective she'd talked to earlier rushed into the barn. "One of the officers mentioned you were here. Didn't know you were involved with this case?"

"Just picking up my girlfriend." Justin's hand moved back to Nikki's hip, subtly steadying her tired legs while marking their relationship. "But we'd appreciate being kept in the loop."

"Of course, sir. I'll make sure you both get all the reports." The detective's posture changed—spine straightening, chin lifting. Nikki had seen this transformation countless times, the instant respect that materialized whenever Justin's rank registered.

She bit back a smile. There was something almost comical about how quickly the detective's tone had shifted. The silver badge effect, she called it. One mention of Justin's name and doors swung open, information flowed freely and reports appeared without the usual dance.

She caught the slight twitch at the corner of Justin's mouth. He never leveraged his position deliberately, but he never corrected the assumption that she worked under his authority either. His fingers pressed gently against her hip, a silent acknowledgment of their unspoken arrangement. And it was a relief to know she wouldn't have to battle bureaucracy for access to the files.

Sure, it occasionally irritated her when people assumed her success came from Justin's influence rather than her own skills. But irritation was acceptable compared to the practical benefits of his rank. And right now, with her body aching and her mind still racing with unanswered questions, any advantage was welcome.

The detective pulled out his notebook, pen poised. "I can brief you on what we've found so far, if you'd like, sir."

Justin nodded, his expression neutral. Another shortcut granted. Nikki shifted her weight, allowing his steady presence to support her while hiding her smile. No qualms about leveraging Justin's position, about the way his badge opened doors that her PI license couldn't. Not a single one.

The detective completed a cursory update and flipped his notebook shut. "I'll have those reports sent over first thing tomorrow, Lieutenant." His gaze slid to Nikki, professional courtesy extending to her by association. "Ms. Drake, thank you. We may need additional statements."

"Not a problem." Nikki kept her voice steady despite her exhaustion. "I'll be available."

Justin whisked her out of the barn and into his car. The familiar comfort of his heated leather seats wrapped around her like a blanket. Gunner sprawled across the back seat, snoring before they even left the property. She fought to keep her eyes open as car lights blurred past, the vehicle's motion nearly lulling her to sleep.

"Tell me about the mountain chase," Justin said, his voice pulling her back. Though he kept his eyes on the road, his concern was obvious. "Sounds like your pursuer didn't want to give up. Most people would have backed off once they lost the target."

She shifted, trying to organize her thoughts through a fog of exhaustion. Justin never tried to interfere, but nights like this had to be hard. A homicide detective who knew exactly how quickly things could go wrong.

"Yes, once Kat was gone, he kept chasing us. That is strange. Doesn't make sense if he was after Conan."

"You think the victim was the target?"

"Or Kat," Nikki said. "But how did the shooter know she was going to keep Conan out on the track? After morning gallops they usually cooled him out by the barn."

"After regular gallops, barn walking is fine," Justin said. "But Kat just put Conan through a serious pre-race work. The kind of effort where a horse's core temperature spikes and they need that long, gradual cool-down. Someone who understood training would know they couldn't just take him straight back to the barn after that type of exertion."

Justin scanned her face in the dashboard light. "Get some sleep," he said. "You can analyze it tomorrow. By the way, if your wonder horse is okay to run Saturday, Tom's agreed to not only give him a stall but also that Rachel can use his pony horse and rider."

Nikki smiled despite her exhaustion. "You believe in Sonja's abilities now? How she knew Conan was misunderstood?"

"I believe in keeping an open mind." His hand found hers in the darkness, fingers intertwining. "And I believe in a determined investigator who never gives up until the job is done."

She wanted to respond, but sleep was pulling her under, her eyes growing heavier with each passing mile. The last thing she registered was Justin's thumb stroking her palm, his quiet strength making her feel safe.

But even as she drifted off, one thought kept circling through her mind: Who really had been the target today?

CHAPTER TWENTY-FOUR

Nikki woke to sunlight streaming through her bedroom window. For a moment she was disoriented, her mind struggling to piece together the night. How had she gotten home? Her last clear memory was being in Justin's car. Everything after that was a blur.

She rolled over, finding empty sheets beside her. Justin had probably gone straight back to his homicide case. Unlike her, he was able to function on minimal sleep, powered by coffee and determination. She'd seen him work two days straight, mind still razor-sharp when others were struggling.

Gunner lifted his head from his bed and gave a groggy tail wag. Her partner had performed flawlessly through the crisis, but even he was showing the toll this morning.

She pushed herself up, every muscle in her body protesting. A glance at her phone showed it was nearly noon. She'd lost hours to an exhaustion-fueled sleep, precious time swallowed by her body's need for recovery. And others were already dealing with the sad aftermath: Sophia's family facing the brutal task of funeral arrangements, crime scene techs processing evidence, Kat and Conan recovering from their ordeal.

A hot shower helped, steam working much of the stiffness from her shoulders. She examined her injuries with professional detachment, the purple bruises blooming along her ribs, scrapes across her arms and legs and raw palms that stung under the water. Each mark carried memories of desperation, of choices made in the dark.

Wrapped in her robe, she moved through her morning routine, muscles loosening with every step. Justin's keys lay on the kitchen counter with a note: *Take my truck today. And get some real sleep. You earned it - J.*

She smiled, touching the keys. Even in a rush, he'd thought of everything. Gunner nudged her leg, reminding her that some routines couldn't wait. She slid open the back door, watching him trot into the fenced yard, relieved to see his normal fluid gait.

Her phone showed a cluster of messages—Rachel, Sonja, even Ashley Robart. But first, coffee. She needed caffeine to help process the tangle of events: Sophia's murder, the mountain pursuit, the strange connection between Kat and Ashley. Most importantly, she needed to understand why their pursuer had seemed more interested in silencing humans than stopping a horse from racing.

Rachel's call came first, anxiety clear in her voice despite obvious attempts to sound positive. "The vet's coming at two. Conan seems fine, but I'm not sure if it's fair to ask him to race on Saturday. Kat insists he can handle it. I just don't know."

"How's Kat doing?" Nikki asked, wrapping her hands around the warmth of her coffee mug.

"Sleeping like a log." Rachel's voice softened, maternal concern overriding worry about a horse. "I can't believe how brave you were. How you found her in those mountains. Without you..."

"Ashley helped," Nikki said, deflecting the gratitude. "Told me about the trailhead outside the police cordon. And about the meadow."

"She always was Kat's friend. It's too bad she lost interest in riding. I know Kat misses her." Rachel sighed. "Everyone has been so amazing through all this. You and Gunner, Ashley, even Jim. But he's devastated about Sophia's death. Says he's selling the facility and moving to Australia. I didn't even know the property had been listed."

Nikki just sipped her coffee and listened while Rachel detailed the current police search—two K9 teams working the trails, no signs of the shooter. The lack of physical evidence bothered her. Their pursuer had known how to avoid leaving traces.

When she hung up, a text from Sonja caught her eye: *Check Mike Jensen's blog. The tide is turning.*

DERBY CONTENDER SHOWS TRUE GRIT *by* Mike Jensen

The controversial colt Conan proved his mettle yesterday in a dramatic display of both athletic ability and devotion to his teenage rider. After fleeing an assassin's bullet, the horse—that had never before encountered ungroomed terrain—carried his rider safely through mountain wilderness with the skill of a seasoned trail horse.

More impressive than his athleticism was his intelligence and heart. When faced with treacherous conditions, Conan remained steady and responsive to his young rider. Sources say he navigated narrow mountain trails with remarkable sure-footedness while maintaining the courage and fighting spirit that makes Thoroughbreds unique.

This kind of adaptability and level-headedness directly contradicts earlier reports about the colt's rebellious nature. A horse capable of protecting his rider through a life-threatening crisis is no savage outlaw. Rather, Conan has shown himself to be that rare combination of raw talent and exceptional mind that defines truly great horses.

This writer hopes the remarkable animal will be cleared to compete Saturday. His presence would add both drama and inspiration to the Santa Anita Derby. And this time, I'll be cheering for him.

The blog was notably different from Jensen's usual style. No anonymous sources casting doubt, no carefully quoted "veteran horsemen" suggesting scandal. Instead of hinting at drugs or danger, his tone radiated admiration. Like someone who'd finally chosen truth over sensationalism.

Nikki closed the browser tab and fingered her mug. Jensen's change of perspective confirmed what she'd witnessed firsthand—Conan's remarkable steadiness under pressure. But she needed more than just public vindication. She needed to figure out who'd been the real target. The horse, as everyone assumed, or something far more disturbing.

Ashley answered on the first ring when Nikki called, her words tumbling out in a rush of concern. "Are Kat and Conan okay? I've been so worried."

"They're both fine," Nikki said. "Thanks for telling me about the trailhead. And where to look for that meadow. You made all the difference."

"Glad I could help. I'm going to call Kat. Wish her luck."

Something had shifted in Ashley's voice, a steadiness replacing the fragile hesitation that had characterized past conversations. Nikki cataloged this subtle change, adding it to the collection of transformations unfolding around Conan.

She opened the patio door. Gunner trotted inside, nails clicking against the kitchen floor just as her phone buzzed. Justin calling.

"Got something interesting," he said. "The trajectory analysis from the rail suggests a skilled marksman. Professional grade shot from that distance and angle. Techs think it had to be an expensive long-range rifle. Not something you'd find at the local gun shop."

"Professional shooter?" Nikki asked, her mind racing through implications. Maybe it was the same people who took Sonny."

"Or someone who really knows their weapons," Justin said. "Could be a serious hunter, or a competition shooter. Whoever it was, they knew what they were doing. How are you feeling?"

"Better every hour." She watched Gunner lap noisily from his water bowl. "Everyone's focused on Conan being the target. But if the shooter was an expert, maybe the bullet that killed Sophia wasn't a mistake."

"Trust your instincts. They're usually right." They both turned silent, a pause filled with shared understanding. "Listen," he added. "I've got to head into a meeting. Probably have time to get your car tomorrow."

"Sounds good. Thanks for last night."

"Always, Nic," he said, his voice gruff with emotion he rarely showed. That single syllable—Nic—carried a tenderness reserved for moments when they were alone.

She ended the call, smiling at her phone. Then quickly sobered. Everything was shifting: alliances, stories, suspicions. She'd seen cases turn like this, when the obvious answer blinded people to darker truths.

Only one thing felt certain: The killer wasn't finished. And she was beginning to fear they were all looking in the wrong direction.

CHAPTER TWENTY-FIVE

Nikki gripped the truck's steering wheel, still adjusting to the Ram's heavier handling. Traffic stretched toward downtown Los Angeles in endless rows of bumpers. From this height, the commute looked like a slow-motion ballet rather than the usual frustrating crawl.

Beside her, Gunner surveyed his kingdom through the wide window. His ears pricked as he looked down at each passing vehicle. He clearly approved of sitting in the passenger's seat, even though she missed her car's nimble responsiveness.

Justin had chosen the truck for practical reasons: high clearance, good visibility, cargo capacity. She preferred vehicles that could slip through traffic and park anywhere. The type that could blend into the background during surveillance.

A motorcycle cut across three lanes, missing their bumper by inches. Nikki's hand moved instinctively toward a nonexistent horn button. Wrong vehicle, wrong spot. She wanted to get her car back soon, though seeing Gunner's enjoyment of his elevated seat almost made the more cumbersome drive worthwhile.

Traffic thinned as they approached her office. She scanned the street, already anticipating the parking challenge. Her usual spot behind the building would be tight. The truck's cab might not even clear the overhang.

"Down, boy," she said as Gunner's tail thumped against the seat. He settled immediately, but he gave an impatient whine, keen to reach the office. They were both energized after their long sleep, though she still had occasional muscle twinges, and likely he did as well.

Gravel crunched beneath her tires as she executed an impatient three-point turn then wedged the truck against the side of the alley. That would have to do.

Sonja's office was dark as Nikki and Gunner walked down the hall. No surprise. Her friend had shifted her psychic readings to remote sessions, preferring to work from her small ranch where she could tend to her rescue animals and Ginger could run free. The arrangement suited both Sonja and her growing client list, though Nikki missed their impromptu coffee breaks.

She unlocked her office and headed to the desk while Gunner trotted past, performing his usual security sweep before settling on his dog bed. She gave his head a pat, knowing nothing had changed in two days, but they both needed the familiar routine.

She booted up her computer, automatically checking her backup files. Cases might pause for mountain chases and murders, but clients still expected their reports. A stack of unfiled receipts caught her eye, along with three invoices she'd meant to finalize. Those mundane tasks felt rather comforting after yesterday's drama.

Her phone buzzed, a text from Sonja: *Working with new owner. Found some interesting patterns. Lots of stressed racehorses with room to improve. When you have time, want to compare notes?*

Nikki typed a quick reply, appreciating how Sonja balanced her genuine gift with professional discretion. No questions about Conan or yesterday's events, just a subtle offer to share insights.

Their different approaches to problems often yielded surprising results, uncovering truths neither would have found alone.

The official police report arrived via encrypted email. She opened the attached photos first, trying for professional detachment but failing miserably. Images of Sophia hit hard—a young woman's life ended without warning. It hurt to see someone cut down so callously, especially someone barely starting their adult life.

She turned to the clinical black and white report:

Report: Mountain View Training Center

Time of Death: Approximately 0730 Victim: Sophia Mendez, age 22 Cause: Single GSW to temporal region Location: Main training track, SE quarter

Initial Findings:

Victim was mounted on gray gelding at time of impact. Two shots fired: First struck rail approximately eight inches from victim's position. Second shot struck victim one inch below riding helmet, resulting in immediate fatality. Trajectory analysis indicates shots fired from elevated position. Distance estimated 150-175 yards, based on ballistics. Shooter location: Likely hillside overlooking SE section of track. No casings recovered.

The report included precise measurements and coordinates but Detective Archie Mason's preliminary analysis caught her eye: *Initial evidence suggests professional execution rather than opportunistic attack. Shooter demonstrated advanced marksmanship skills and intimate knowledge of facility layout. First shot appears deliberately placed to create specific reaction in horse/rider, positioning victim for fatal second shot.*

Nikki pulled in a resigned breath, focusing on the bullet's path through the rail near the half-mile pole. The angle wasn't what she'd expected. It came from higher than a vehicle or ground position would allow. The shooter had chosen a spot that offered both elevation and clear sight lines to the track's most isolated section.

The detective's notes continued. *Primary suspects include: Saudi representatives (documented threats, military training probable); James Wellington connections (motive established, resources available); Unknown racing industry players (betting and breeding implications)*

She scanned the footnote about Jim Turner's statement: *Witness observed from specialized van parked at opposite side of track. Reports seeing two men in dark clothing fleeing between barns. Unable to provide detailed description due to distance/angle. Note: Witness's location provides alibi for time of shooting.*

Nikki rubbed her forehead, trying to make sense of the scene. Jim's van had been the lone vehicle close to the rail. Rolf had directed all other traffic to the parking lot behind the grandstand. That would explain Jim witnessing two men running between the barns. But the fatal shot had come from elevation. The men would have been noticed if they climbed the slope. And if they'd been on the hillside, why run back to the barn area?

She opened her case document and added new notes. Connecting Threads:

Ashley witnesses Jim's accident. Stops riding completely. Sophia works closely with Jim, starts dating him after accident. Sophia dies, shot by accomplished shooter from high ground. Jim shows minimal grief, plans to sell and move to Australia. Two separate incidents: Sophia's murder and mountain pursuit? Connection between Ashley and Kat, both avoid Jim. Kat's protective behavior around her mother.

The pieces were there, scattered like puzzle fragments, but Nikki still couldn't see the full picture. She kept circling back to Kat and her reaction whenever Jim appeared. Her aversion seemed to extend far beyond normal teenage behavior.

Her phone's buzz yanked her from her thoughts. A text from Ashley: *Ready to talk. About the day Mr. Turner was hurt and about Sophia. Can you come by after school sometime?*

Nikki jerked forward, her optimism rising as she reread the message. Teenagers often spotted what adults overlooked, their youthful perspectives uncluttered by years of assumptions and expectations. While everyone else fixated on the obvious, Ashley might know something more significant.

She typed an immediate reply, confirming she'd come today. She had a growing suspicion that Sophia's murder had nothing to do with Conan. But she needed a breakthrough, a nugget of information that would help everything else fall into place.

And Ashley's careful wording suggested the girl might hold that critical piece.

CHAPTER TWENTY-SIX

Nikki maneuvered Justin's truck through the modest neighborhood where Ashley lived, the afternoon sun casting long shadows across patchy lawns. Her house looked different today—less secretive, more tired. Scattered toys dotted the yard, and a basketball sat against the wall where someone had recently abandoned their game.

She checked her watch. Just after three. Gunner shifted in the seat, tail wagging as kids streamed past on the sidewalk. School buses were dropping off students, parents arriving home from work. Normal routines playing out while she tried to put a name on a killer. Not just a name, but his driving motive. And if Conan hadn't been the actual target, then who? And why?

Ashley opened the door before Nikki could ring the bell, one hand smoothing the front of her oversized shirt. "Can we talk in the backyard?" she asked. "Mom's got the little ones watching TV."

Nikki followed her through a narrow side gate into a small yard dominated by a crooked swing set. The space felt intimate, protected from prying eyes by tall wooden fencing and overgrown shrubs.

Ashley settled onto one of the swings, her feet scuffing the dirt. Gunner lay down nearby, positioning himself to watch both gate and house.

"You asked about this before," Ashley finally said. "And I didn't tell the truth. Was too ashamed. But after what just happened, it's not right to keep quiet." She swallowed and fell silent. Birds called from the trees and a dog barked in a nearby yard, but Nikki waited, giving her time.

Ashley squeezed the swing chains so tightly her knuckles whitened. "I didn't want anyone to know," she said. "Everyone thinks Conan spooked and ran Jim down. That's what Kat and I told the police. But it wasn't like that."

She visibly swallowed then the words tumbled out. "Mr. Turner, he was always watching us, the young riders. Making excuses to help with our riding. Giving us special attention. I just thought he was being nice. I was so stupid. But Kat knew better. She saw how he was when no one else was around.

"That morning I was bathing Sonny between the two barns. Mr. Turner cornered me. Said I was his favorite rider, that he could help my career. He hugged me, stuck his hand down my pants, touched me..." She shook her head, her slim body shuddering with revulsion.

"Kat saw everything from Conan's back." The swing creaked faster, chains protesting, but Ashley kept talking. "She didn't hesitate. Just rode straight for him. She knew exactly what she was doing. So did Conan. That horse, he was like her partner. His hooves didn't touch me. Then Jim was on the ground. It looked like it could have been an accident. So I made her promise not to tell the truth."

She looked at Nikki, her eyes haunted. "So it's my fault Conan got that reputation. I made everything harder, and they've always been so nice to me. Rachel was the one who convinced Sonny's owner to let me ride her horse." Her voice hardened. "But I won't press charges. I don't want anyone to ever know. Not my mom, not the police. No one. Promise you won't tell?"

Nikki nodded, swallowing back the sour taste in her throat. Her hands fisted as memories of her sister surfaced. So young, also targeted by a predator who'd used his power to isolate and control. That familiar rage burned hot, but these moments weren't about her anger. They were about supporting the young woman in front of her, who'd finally found the courage to speak.

"It wasn't your fault," Nikki said, clearing her throat. "None of it. Jim is solely to blame. And Conan and his connections are doing fine." She tilted her head, professional instincts cutting through personal fury. "You think Jim had something to do with Sophia's shooting?"

"No, not really. But Sophia was always hanging around, like she was obsessed. Would do anything to get his attention. Maybe he got tired of it and wanted more of a challenge." Ashley looked up at Nikki, her face bleak. "And she hated the way he looked at Rachel. Everyone could see Jim still loved her."

Nikki nodded. She'd noticed it too.

"Sophia called me sometimes," Ashley continued. "Boring calls, always worried that Jim and Rachel would get back together. He was all she wanted to talk about."

The back door slammed and Ashley half-rose, shoulders stiffening until she saw her little brother race past with a soccer ball. "Mom's probably wondering where I am," she murmured, but her hands remained wrapped around the swing chains.

"Is there anything else I should know?" Nikki kept her voice gentle, instinct telling her that Ashley wasn't finished. "Anything that would help Kat and Rachel?"

"Just that Sophia changed. Started talking different, cocky. Said she'd be moving away soon. Like she finally had some influence with Jim."

Nikki waited, letting Ashley work through her thoughts. Afternoon shadows had crept across the small yard, touching the rusty swing set. From a distant house, a mother's voice called kids in for dinner.

"And Kat," Ashley went on, her voice twisted with pain. "I talked to her today. She blames herself for not speaking up. She says we can trust you. Thinks maybe Sophia would still be alive if we'd told the truth."

"None of this is Kat's fault. Or yours. You were both teenagers dealing with an adult predator."

"I know. But Kat's changed too. She used to love riding. Now she stays close to her mother, always watching for Jim." She wrapped a strand of hair around her finger. "Sophia thought Kat was trying to keep them apart—Rachel and Jim. But I don't think it was just that. Kat's afraid of him. And after how she put him in a wheelchair, she probably should be."

Her words came faster, as if she needed to get them out. "Jim goes after what he wants. Maybe Sophia found that out too late. All I know for sure is that I never want to see him again."

She abruptly stood, the empty swing jerking behind her. It was clear she was finished talking. Finished revealing secrets that had shaped months of silence. Secrets that still held the power to hurt.

"Thank you for telling me," Nikki said, rising from beside the swing set. "I know it wasn't easy."

Ashley nodded, already retreating toward her house. But her shoulders were straighter than they'd been last week, as if carrying less weight.

Nikki trudged through the side gate to the truck, Ashley's revelations heavy on her mind. She fumbled with the key before managing to unlock the door. Another predator hiding behind respectability. Another young girl traumatized while adults remained oblivious. Her rage bubbled. Not just for Ashley, but for all victims who suffered in silence.

She knew the stats, the reality that Ashley would likely never bring charges. By the time most victims found their voice, evidence had faded and memories blurred. Predators like Jim counted on that, on shame keeping their secrets safe while they abused new targets. She motioned for Gunner to jump in then slid behind the wheel, taking several calming breaths before starting the engine.

She had just pulled out of the subdivision when her phone buzzed with a text from Rachel: *Vet cleared Conan to race! Having small celebration at barn. Come by if you can.*

Nikki grimaced, not at all in the mood for a celebration. But she was so close to Mountain View. And after everything that had happened, and what she'd just learned, Conan deserved his chance at glory. The horse had turned out to be the most innocent one of all.

Traffic was light on the country road, giving her time to think. Everything she'd observed took on new meaning—Jim's constant presence at the track during Kat's workouts, his surprisingly quick recovery after Sophia's death, his sudden plans to leave the country. Now each piece carried darker significance.

She turned into the center's drive where vehicles filled the small parking area. Fortunately there were no police cars. Only fragments of yellow tape remained, fluttering from posts like tired streamers.

Music and laughter drifted from the barn, a welcome change from yesterday's sirens. The festive atmosphere hit her as she paused in the doorway. Someone had strung holiday lights along the center aisle, their warm glow softening the barn's shadows. Conan's head hung over his stall door, a full participant in the unusual activity. A folding table held cookies and lemonade, though Marco hovered nearby, ever vigilant about keeping treats restricted to humans.

"Nikki!" Rachel hurried over, followed closely by a grinning Kat. Other than some scratches on her arms and face, Kat showed no evidence of yesterday's ordeal. "The vet says Conan's fine," Rachel said. "Good appetite, sound, perfect blood work. So he's going to run!"

"That's wonderful." Nikki glanced toward the office building, roughly two hundred yards away. Jim's specialized van was parked there, marking his absence from the celebration.

"Jim couldn't come," Rachel said, following Nikki's gaze. "He doesn't feel much like celebrating. And he needs to prepare for a meeting at the realtor's office tomorrow."

Nikki relaxed, glad she wouldn't have to face him. It would be impossible to hide her revulsion. She'd felt his eyes on her before, his calculating dislike. Even during casual conversations, he tracked expressions, cataloging reactions. That talent likely served him well when selecting victims, identifying which girls might stay silent. Now, knowing what she did, every part of her would recoil. And Jim, with his predator's instinct, would notice.

"We're shipping to Santa Anita tomorrow morning," Rachel went on. "Justin's trainer has his stall ready though Jim offered to let us stay here through Friday. Thought his security guard could protect Conan better than the track."

"The track is safer," Nikki said quickly. Her mind kept circling back to Ashley's revelations, Jim's predatory nature, his hatred for Kat. Could he have made that shot from his van? Doubtful. The trajectory was wrong. But she was determined to check the grandstand area in daylight, ideally when he wasn't around.

"What time is Jim's meeting tomorrow?" Nikki asked, keeping her voice casual. "Will he be able to see Conan off?"

"Yes, his meeting isn't until one. Unfortunately his realtor thinks the shooting will affect the sale price. She wants to discuss improvements that might help. Better security systems, enhanced lighting and a road monitor."

Nikki nodded, struggling to keep her expression neutral. She eased away from Rachel as her phone buzzed. A text from Justin: *Police obtained search warrant for Wellington's records. Nothing suspicious in financials or phone records. Dead end.*

She stared at the message, wondering if she'd been focused on the wrong suspects. Wellington, the Saudis, the obvious threats. If Jim wasn't in a wheelchair, would she have considered him capable of murder? The answer left her chilled.

She'd never questioned his paralysis before. But now everything seemed suspicious—his pending insurance payout, Sophia's cocky attitude before her death and how Jim always managed to be positioned to witness crucial events. She needed to investigate his background, dig deeper into that insurance claim and check the sight lines from his office and his van.

Most importantly, she needed to know what Sophia had discovered that made her so confident. And if that knowledge had cost the young woman her life.

CHAPTER TWENTY-SEVEN

Nikki stared at her office phone, rehearsing her approach. Dawn had barely broken, shading the street below in gunmetal gray. Even Vinny's restaurant sat quiet, though hints of garlic and yeast drifted up from their patio, promising delicious fresh-baked bread. Gunner dozed on his bed, unfazed by their early start. Like always, he trusted her judgment about when their day should begin.

She'd spent much of last night researching medical terminology until her eyes burned from the screen's glare. Case studies on spinal trauma, recovery patterns and sensation-testing protocols. She'd absorbed it all, committing key phrases to memory. If she was going to impersonate a physician to investigate Jim's insurance claim, her performance had to be flawless.

The insurance company would expect the doctor to be familiar with every aspect of spinal cord injuries—reflex responses, dermatome mapping, motor function assessment. One wrong term, one telling hesitation, and they might start asking their own questions.

Five million dollars was a powerful motive for fraud. If Jim had been faking his paralysis, there should be inconsistencies in his medical evaluations. Paperwork that didn't quite match. Assessment patterns that deviated from the standard. She just needed access to those records, access no private investigator would ever be granted.

She pressed the number to Westward Mutual's claims division, using the direct line she'd obtained yesterday. Her heart pounded against her ribs while she waited. Two rings, then a brisk female voice answered. "Claims Assessment, this is Barbara."

"Good morning." Nikki adopted the crisp, slightly impatient tone of a busy doctor juggling too many cases. "Dr. Sarah Chen here, consulting on James Turner's case. We're short staffed and I need to verify some neurological findings for a co-worker's report."

Papers shuffled on the other end. "Of course, Doctor. I have Mr. Turner's file right here."

"We seem to be missing the pain response summary from his initial exam." Nikki forced her voice to maintain its professional edge along with a harried tone, like someone calling between patients. "Do your files show the tests?"

"Oh yes, very thorough. The attending physician noted complete absence of sensation from L1 down. No response to deep pressure or pinprick stimulation."

"None at all? Even with maximum pressure points?"

"Nothing. It's all documented here. Multiple tests, different stimuli. Complete paralysis consistent with the trauma described."

"And these findings were consistent across all exams?"

"Absolutely. Reports all confirm complete loss of sensation." Barbara's tone grew curious. "Is there some question about the diagnosis?"

"No, just being thorough with the paperwork." Nikki steered toward safer territory before the woman's curiosity could deepen. "And the anticipated settlement date?"

"Should be finalized by the end of the week." Pride crept into Barbara's voice. "One of our largest payouts this year."

Nikki ended the call before leaning back in her chair and letting her shoulders slump. The medical evidence seemed clear. It couldn't have been Jim chasing them through those mountains. Though that didn't rule him out for Sophia's murder. Part of her admitted she wanted him to be guilty, that Ashley's revelations had colored her perspective.

But if Jim's paralysis was real, that only eliminated him as their physical pursuer. It didn't clear him of arranging Sophia's murder, or sending someone to hunt them down. She had a burning desire to connect him to those crimes, a visceral need that went beyond professional duty.

She'd seen too many predators walk free, their victims left without justice or closure. Men who targeted vulnerable girls, who used their position and charm to groom and manipulate. The memory of Ashley's haunted eyes, the way Kat stiffened whenever Jim appeared—these weren't coincidences. They were warning signs, the same ones that had surrounded her sister before she disappeared.

Nikki set the phone down, acknowledging the emotional pull that could only cloud her judgment. She needed evidence, not just righteous anger. If Jim had arranged Sophia's murder, if he'd sent someone after Kat, there'd be proof. And she intended to find it.

Predators like Jim Turner didn't deserve second chances. And they certainly didn't deserve five million dollars to start fresh in another country.

Her regular databases yielded dozens of Jim Turners, far too many to easily narrow down. She even tried a specialized veterans' archive, but nothing relevant appeared. The only clear hit was from old 4H records. A grainy photo showed a teenage Jim accepting a trophy for best-groomed dairy cow at the county fair. His proud smile matched the one she'd seen in more recent photos hanging in Mountain View's office.

A deeper search turned up mentions of him in local farm reports and Future Farmers of America newsletters. The picture that emerged was of a country kid who'd grown up raising livestock, showing animals, working the land. Nothing sinister, nothing suggesting expertise with weapons. Though growing up rural usually meant familiarity with guns.

She pulled up Mountain View's property maps on her screen, studying the elevation changes between the office and the spot close to the grandstand where Jim had parked his van. The topography was almost completely flat with barely a foot of variation across the entire area. There was no way someone in a wheelchair could have made that shot. The trajectory had clearly come from much higher.

She pushed her chair back and grabbed her keys. Ashley's revelations about Jim's predatory nature didn't automatically make him a murderer. But before ruling him out, she needed to check those sight lines. Make sure the maps were accurate.

Gunner scrambled to his feet, sensing her urgency. She checked her watch. 9:47 am. Jim's realtor meeting was at one o'clock. Plenty of time to drive to Mountain View and check out the area while he was gone.

Morning traffic had thinned, and she made good time in Justin's truck. Her elevated position gave a different perspective on the route. As she neared the training center, she found herself studying each hill and ridgeline with fresh eyes, noting potential vantage points and natural cover. Places where someone intimate with the local terrain could set up without being seen.

Gunner's eager whine filled the cab when they turned into the parking lot, though he was likely disappointed by the lack of activity. No horses circled the track, no grooms called friendly greetings. But it was the quiet time of day when most horses dozed in their stalls. She'd never visited during these hours, but as she'd hoped, Jim's van was missing from its usual spot near the office.

Her hatchback sat alone in front of Conan's vacated barn, looking small and exposed. Amazing how different everything felt from last night's celebration. The festive lights were gone, the laughter silenced, replaced by the stillness of abandoned space. But along with the drowsy quiet came the perfect chance to investigate.

She parked the truck alongside her car then hurried along the horse path to the gap, her boots sinking into the deep footing. No wonder she never saw Jim on these paths. The soft dirt would make rolling a wheelchair impossible. Gunner moved ahead, his relaxed trot confirming they were alone. Still, she was comforted by her Glock tucked in her backpack.

The office building cast a short shadow beneath the noon sun. She paused in its shade, studying angles and distances. From this position, the backstretch presented a clear shot for anyone with a decent rifle and basic skill. But the police report had been explicit. Both bullets, the one retrieved from Sophia and the one lodged in the rail, had been fired from an elevated angle. The shooter had to have been positioned higher.

She pulled out her binoculars and scanned the area by the half-mile pole where the rail had been damaged. Someone had removed the yellow tape, probably worried it would spook galloping horses, but she could still see where Sophia had fallen.

The angle of entry through the splintered rail confirmed what the report said. The shots had come from height.

She followed the outer rail to the spot where Jim's vehicle had been parked. The van's tinted windows would have provided cover. Maybe he'd parked here to establish his presence, create an alibi, without actually being inside.

But the steep ridge behind the track posed an obvious problem. Even if Jim could somehow roll his wheelchair up that incline, which seemed impossible, a man carrying a rifle would have drawn attention. The grandstand had been dotted with spectators, all gathered to watch Conan's work.

She tilted her head, staring at the tree-covered hill. Jim might have had help. Maybe an accomplice had hidden the weapon up there, when the facility was empty. Someone capable of climbing that hill, hiding a rifle, making that shot.

Could it have been Rolf? He had military training, weapons expertise, the physical ability. Her stomach roiled at the thought. Gunner had trusted the guard instantly, a response her dog reserved for people with genuine integrity. She'd watched them together, how her normally cautious Shepherd had melted under his touch, those gentle hands finding exactly the right spot behind his ears. The possibility that they'd both been deceived felt like betrayal on multiple levels.

She trudged up the hill, throat tight. The police had conducted an extensive search with their K9 teams yesterday. But she wasn't used to relying on other investigations, needed to see for herself. And if Rolf had hidden there with that rifle, Gunner would know. His nose remembered people long after they'd gone.

She couldn't believe Rolf was involved. But she'd been wrong before.

CHAPTER TWENTY-EIGHT

Nikki worked her way along the ridge, scanning the terrain. The track spread below like an artist's sketch, sun highlighting the white rails. It was understandable why a sniper would choose this spot. Clear sight lines and good concealment with multiple escape routes through the trees. There was even a flag, showing wind direction.

The ridge itself formed a natural shooting platform, a granite outcropping creating an ideal rest for a rifle. Pine needles carpeted the ground, now riddled with investigators' footprints. But there was no sign of compressed earth where someone might have lain in wait. No trace of a killer's presence.

She checked on Gunner who was working out in a spiral pattern, nose close to the ground. His body language told her he wasn't picking up anything suspicious. No lingering scent of gunpowder or gun oil. And no scent of a man he considered a friend.

She blew out a sigh of relief and continued checking spots where someone might have stashed a weapon. Maybe the police had found something they weren't sharing. More likely she was grasping at straws, too eager to find evidence that would implicate Jim.

Half an hour later, she had to accept that the ridge was the perfect sniper's nest, but it hadn't been used to kill Sophia. Not by Jim or Rolf or anyone else.

The office building drew her gaze. Solid, ordinary, well positioned to survey the facility, its wide windows resembling watching eyes. From here, she could see what looked like a tiny attic above the main floor, more crawl space than a room. High enough to explain the bullet's trajectory? Maybe.

She hurried back down the hill and circled to the front of the office. The doorknob turned smoothly but remained locked. The lock itself was unexpected. Not the simple deadbolt she'd expected, but a sophisticated electronic system more suited to a bank than a training facility. Her lock picks would be useless against this level of security.

Basic business records shouldn't require that kind of protection. Maybe it was about privacy. She'd already learned that Jim had dirty secrets. Maybe he brought young riders here. She circled the building, looking for other access, but found every window securely locked, their frames reinforced. Her suspicions deepened with each new security measure.

Then she spotted it—a small screened window set high in the back wall. It looked almost like an afterthought, designed for ventilation before central air had been installed. But unlike the other features, the screen appeared new. The aluminum frame was still bright, untouched by weather or corrosion.

She pulled out her binoculars, studying it more closely. The screen itself looked spotless, lacking the usual dust that gathered on exterior fixtures. The window sat a good twelve feet up, but Justin's truck might provide enough height. Its elevated cab stood at least six feet tall. If she could position it directly beneath the window, the roof might give her enough height to grab the ledge.

The ground behind the building sloped unevenly, scattered with rocks and clumps of tall grass that would make precise parking a challenge. Still, she could probably get the truck close enough to make the attempt.

She jogged back to the truck, urged Gunner inside then drove to the rear of the office, using four-wheel drive to edge over the uneven ground. After a bit of maneuvering, she was able to position the vehicle mere inches from the back wall. Now the pristine screen above her head gleamed like an invitation.

"Stay," she told Gunner, who settled onto the seat with a reluctant grunt. But his concerned eyes tracked her every movement and he whined in protest when she began to climb out the truck window.

"It's okay, boy," she whispered, though the reassurance felt hollow. If something about this office triggered his protective response, there was probably good reason. But this first climb was nothing more than an experiment, determining if entry was even possible. The height alone presented a challenge, with minimal handholds on the weathered siding. Even if she managed to reach the window, its narrow opening might be too small for her body.

She eased out the truck window and onto the edge of the hood, testing each step before shifting her weight. Then she worked her way up to the cab's roof. The window was a stretch, but manageable. And the screen came away with surprising ease, its shiny screws turning easily, as if they'd been recently loosened.

Gripping the window ledge, she tested its strength before pulling herself up. The opening was tight. She'd have to slip in, head first, and hope for a solid landing on the other side. But so far, it seemed like a go. However as she balanced there, the significance of Gunner's concern made her pause. If Jim had killed Sophia, he was more dangerous than she'd imagined.

And what if Jim had somehow been their pursuer in the mountains? That would explain Gunner's concern. It might also explain why Jim had avoided last night's barn celebration, making excuses about grief when he'd shown little actual distress over Sophia's death. Maybe he'd been avoiding Gunner, knowing the dog would react to his scent, connecting him to the mountains in a way humans couldn't.

She dropped back to the roof of the truck while Gunner continued to whine from inside the cab. "Just in case," she said, reaching through the open window and pulling the Glock from her pack. She wasn't taking any chances.

Not after everything she'd learned about Jim Turner.

CHAPTER TWENTY-NINE

Nikki wiggled headfirst through the tiny window, gun secured in her back waistband. The space beyond lay in shadows, the air heavy with dust. She flattened her hands over what felt like exposed beams then rose to a crouch.

She pulled out her phone, sweeping its flashlight beam across her surroundings. She was in a crawl space, barely four feet high at its peak. The beam she crouched on was one of several crossing the ceiling of the office below. Cobwebs draped the rafters on both sides, undisturbed for years. But the area between the window and what appeared to be a trap door was suspiciously clear.

Her light caught something else—fresh scuff marks on the adjacent beam. Her breathing quickened as she peered closer. These weren't random marks; they had the distinctive pattern of something long pressed against the surface. Could they have been left by someone bracing a rifle, lying steady for a shot?

She crept along the wooden beams, testing each one before shifting her weight, intent now on reaching the trap door. But the sharp odor of machine oil mingled with the musty attic dust, creating a combination that made her nose itch. Her sudden sneeze echoed alarmingly in the confined space.

She gave her nose an impatient rub and panned her light over the trap door. Its hinges gleamed with oil and when she gripped the handle, the door lifted in silence—the meticulous work of someone who valued stealth.

She peered through the opening, noting it was a good ten-foot drop to the hardwood floor. Not the kind of descent anyone would want to make, and certainly not a man confined to a wheelchair.

She played her light around the corners of the office. No rope, no ladder, nothing to suggest how anyone would access the crawl space. Yet those scuff marks were fresh and the path to the trap door swept clean. There had to be a way.

Her eyes narrowed on the reception desk, slightly offset from the trap door. An athletic person could use the desk and then pull themselves up. And if she lowered herself and swung left, she'd be able to land on the top. She wasn't going to pass up this chance to search Jim's office. He might have child porn or some other evidence of youth exploitation. That would put him away, even if she couldn't pin him to Sophia's murder.

Encouraged, she eased feet first through the opening, clinging onto the wooden edge with the tips of her fingers. She swung left, thumped onto the desk and dropped to the floor. Then she hurried around the divider separating Jim's private space from the reception area.

The top drawer of his desk yielded nothing but standard office supplies and several packs of mint gum. The second drawer contained a stack of documents: routine paperwork like Coggins test results and Consent to Call a Vet forms. She found binoculars, phone chargers, and a collection of recent blog clippings, mostly by Mike Jensen. So Jim could have been Jensen's source. Scummy behavior, but hardly damning.

The third drawer was locked. A quick search revealed no key, but the simple pin and tumbler lock gave way to a handy paper clip within thirty seconds. She heard a satisfying click and the drawer slid open.

A box of condoms lay on top, surprising for a supposedly paralyzed man. Maybe Sophia had been cramping his style. People had been killed for less. She dug deeper, finding more papers, signed waivers and several photographs. Two showed a large buck with impressive antlers. The third picture held her attention, the San Felipe win photo.

Rachel stood beaming beside Conan and his jockey, but the rest of the picture had been cut away, removing everyone else, including Marco and Kat. The mutilation spoke volumes about Jim's feelings for Rachel, his determination to edit reality to his liking. No wonder he'd kept this locked away from Sophia.

At the bottom of the drawer lay a security log detailing Rolf Olsen's routines along with a handwritten note that he could use the apartment in the end barn and have access to coffee in the office at night. She paused, wondering again if Rolf could be involved. He certainly had the shooting skills.

The security log confirmed Rolf was off duty in the day, not starting until eight pm. The timing could have allowed him to be in the mountains for much of the pursuit. And would anyone have noticed if he was late for his night shift? She pulled out her phone, needing to check if he had an alibi.

Rachel answered on the first ring. "Everything's fine here," Rachel said. "Conan's settled in his stall. He has both hay nets and the salt blocks. There's a stable pony here called Sugar who keeps wanting to visit. Sonja says that's a good sign."

"Sugar recognizes good horses," Nikki said, smiling despite her focus on the security log. Sugar's interest was definitely worth noting. The horses he escorted on the track had a higher than usual win percentage. Sonja had all sorts of theories about the reason, but right now Nikki needed information. "Must be quite a change from all the drama at Mountain View," she added, keeping her voice light. "By the way, was Rolf with you when Sophia was shot?"

"Yes, right beside me at the gap. And then he stayed up manning the office, but you know how responsible ex-military guys are. He spent the whole day organizing food for the police, making sure they had what they needed." Rachel paused. "Why do you ask?"

"Just piecing things together." Nikki's grip relaxed and she shoved the security log back in the drawer. "What about Jim? I thought he arranged for the food?"

"He paid for it. But he was too devastated to stick around. He went back to his house. Wanted to be alone." Rachel's voice softened. "A couple of his hunting buddies called when they heard the news, but Jim wasn't taking calls."

Nikki jerked upright. This changed everything. "His friends hunt? Jim too?"

"Oh yes. He was quite passionate about it before the accident." Voices erupted in the background. "Sorry," Rachel said. "Got to run. Feed truck's here and Marco's worried about the exhaust drifting into the barn. I'll call you back."

"No need. I'm planning to stop by later." Nikki cut the connection, charged with excitement. She had enough here to interest the police. More than enough.

Jim's supposed alibi in his van wouldn't hold up against this discovery—he could have taken his shot from this hidden perch then wheeled himself back to the vehicle to play the shocked witness. The trajectory from this crawl space to the rail where

Sophia was shot would fit with the ballistics report. And Rachel had just confirmed he was an experienced hunter.

A sharp bark from outside made her freeze. Then she heard it—the distinctive sound of a vehicle parking by the office door. And her heart sank.

He was back early.

CHAPTER THIRTY

Nikki slammed the drawer shut. Her eyes shot to the trap door above Sophia's desk, now impossibly distant. There were no time to climb back up, and a chair left on the desk would definitely be noticed. Besides, her truck was parked behind the office and Gunner's increasingly frantic barks had already announced her presence.

She rushed back to Sophia's desk and placed the chair back on the floor. Then she sat down, her hand moving behind her back, checking the Glock's position. The weapon was comforting but shooting her way out wasn't an option. Not without justification. Maybe Jim would roll in with a rifle across his lap, making things simple. She could only hope.

For now she maintained the tactical advantage. Her Glock was accessible, her position gave a clear sightline to the door, and most importantly, he had no idea how much she'd discovered. He'd return thinking his secrets were still hidden, unaware she suspected he was more mobile than he pretended, that she knew about his hunting background and that he had no alibi for Sophia's murder. As long as she controlled her reactions, she could keep that edge.

She pulled out her phone, fingers flying over the screen as she speed-dialed Justin. She'd promised him, after a particularly close call, that she'd never knowingly walk into dangerous confrontations without sending him an alert. Working alone had its advantages, but it also meant no backup unless it was created. This qualified as the kind of dicey situation covered by their agreement.

The van's engine cut off just as the call connected. She lowered the volume and tucked the phone beneath a green file folder on Sophia's desk, positioning it so the speaker remained unobstructed. Then she settled behind the desk, angling the chair for a perfect view of the entrance.

Steadying her breathing, she ran through her discoveries. The crawl space access remained a mystery, as did the identity of their mountain pursuer. But she was quite certain of one thing—Jim had killed Sophia, or at least arranged for someone to shoot from the attic. Now she had to be ready for whatever lay beneath his smooth façade.

Wheels rolled along the wooden ramp, the sound unnerving even though he was in a wheelchair and likely unarmed. The electronic lock whirred. Justin's whispered "Nikki?" barely carried from the hidden phone as the door swung wide.

Jim stopped his wheelchair in the doorway, his eyes scanning the office with surprising calm. No rifle was visible, which meant this wouldn't be a simple shoot-out.

"Hey, Jim," she called, projecting her voice to reach Justin's listening phone. Jim's face showed no surprise at finding her there. He simply rolled further into the office and closed the door with practiced efficiency. The lock engaged with a click.

"Hello, Nikki." He tilted his head, his gaze on the open trap door. "I was wondering when you'd figure it out."

"Figure out what?" She tilted her head, gambling on her bluff. "That you really can walk?"

"Among other things. Though I assume you haven't shared that particular detail with anyone yet. Otherwise this would be an official visit."

Outside, Gunner's barking intensified, growing more urgent. "Protective dog." Jim's lips curled into something that wasn't quite a smile. "Bet you wish he was in here with you."

"I always leave him in the vehicle when investigating insurance fraud." She maintained steady eye contact, selling the lie. "He bit someone once and the company wasn't happy. And this *is* an official visit. Westward Mutual hired me to check you out. I used Conan as a reason to hang around the center. Find out if you're really paralyzed."

Her gaze caught a red scratch just visible above his collar, the kind of mark left by a tree branch when rushing through thick forest. Hunting prey.

The room sharpened around her as details crystallized. The ticking of a wall clock, the twitching of Jim's jaw, and the distance between her and the door. She kept her expression blank while her body prepared for fight or flight. He'd all but admitted he could walk. She knew in her gut he'd been there that night.

She forced a soothing smile, giving him a way out. "I still don't know the truth. What to tell the company about your paralysis?"

Jim leaned back, staring at her with eyes that were a bit too intelligent. Nikki kept her bland smile despite Gunner's barks. She'd ordered him to stay, but sometimes his protective instincts overrode commands, especially when he thought she was in danger. Maybe Jim would believe her story and let them drive away. Let the police finish this.

"Nice try," he said. "But I don't believe you. You came for that damn horse. Even Rachel is impressed with your knowledge. So now what am I to do?"

Frantic scratching raked the office door. Gunner had obviously jumped from the truck and circled around to the front. But that door might as well be a fortress wall. Nikki leaned forward, leaving room between her back and the chair, positioning herself to draw the Glock. Neither of them was pretending now.

"I didn't mean for it to be like this." Jim rolled closer, a chilling satisfaction creeping into his voice. "But I'll be glad when Rachel stops talking as if you're her big savior. It's always 'Nikki found this' and 'Nikki suggested that.' Quite tedious, really."

"But you're the one she relies on. She's always grateful for your help. Appreciates everything you've done."

"Appreciates?" He let out a bitter laugh. "You think I want her gratitude? After everything we had? Everything we could have again? I had it all planned. Then you showed up, asking questions, poking around."

"Just trying to protect her horse." Nikki avoided using Conan's name. No need to provoke Jim further by mentioning the animal that had supposedly caused his paralysis. He clearly had some hot buttons.

"You ruined everything!" His nostrils flared. "You and that other bitch."

"Sophia?"

Jim's expression softened, a flicker of something almost like regret crossing his face. "She was a big help. Understood about the insurance money. We were going to take it, start fresh."

"But she changed her mind?" Nikki kept her voice gentle, understanding. "Threatened to expose the fraud?"

His fingers tightened on the wheelchair arms. "I didn't mean to shoot her. Just wanted her out of the office."

"So it was the horse you were aiming for?"

"Not the damn horse." Irritation flashed across Jim's face, his patience clearly wearing thin. "Try to keep up."

"Kat?" Nikki jerked back. Nausea twisted her stomach, a cold sweat breaking across her skin as she connected Ashley's revelations to this new horror.

The pieces aligned with ugly clarity—Jim's hatred, his patience, his willingness to destroy anyone who threatened his desperate scheme.

"That bitch cost me everything," Jim said. "My marriage, my ability to walk. For months I was actually paralyzed because of her and that horse." Raw hatred bled through his words. "But Rachel still loves me. I see it when she looks at me. Without her kid in the way, we can be together again."

Bile rose in her throat. He planned to kill Kat, a child he'd once claimed to care for. She forced herself to maintain eye contact, to keep her voice steady.

"I don't think Rachel would forgive you for murdering her daughter." The words felt filthy in her mouth as she acknowledged his monstrous plan and she fought the trembling that threatened to sweep her body. Everything in her screamed to end this conversation.

"She'll never know. She'll be relieved to move away, far from where her daughter died. I just need another plan." His voice turned accusing. "Because of you."

He was still hunting Kat, even after mistakenly killing an innocent woman. And Nikki had heard enough. She reached back, fingers finding the familiar grip of her Glock.

"You're a creep, a lousy shot, and a coward," she said, no longer hiding her fury. "Chasing Conan and Kat in the mountains. Then running away because you can't handle it when others are armed. Like now."

Her words were precise cuts designed to provoke, to strip away his last pretense of control. She wanted him to show what he really was, to give her justification. Her thumb found the safety, disengaging it with a barely audible click. Then she added, "Rachel could never love scum like you."

For a split second, Jim froze. Then he exploded from the wheelchair with shocking speed, launching himself across the desk in a fluid motion that sent his chair shooting backwards. Papers scattered in the air, her hidden phone clattering to the floor, its connection to Justin still open but now yards away.

They crashed into the filing cabinet, her head slamming against metal. The impact sent a shower of manila folders raining around them as the cabinet rocked backward. His sour coffee breath hit her face as he pinned her against the cold steel, all pretense of disability gone.

Through blurred vision, she saw the rage contorting his face. She drove her knee up, catching him in the gut. He grunted but kept coming. One hand locked around her throat while the other wrestled for her gun. She slammed her elbow into his face, feeling cartilage crunch beneath the blow. But his grip tightened.

Spots danced at the edges of her vision. She jabbed desperately at his eyes with her free hand, heard his pained cry. She leveled the Glock. Heard Gunner's frantic barking through the roaring in her ears, along with a man's shout. Then a dark missile of fur and fury launched between them, blocking her shot.

Gunner's jaws closed on Jim's arm, dragging him sideways. She rolled clear, gasping for breath. Saw Jim slam his fist into Gunner's ribs. Her dog yelped but maintained his grip. She straightened, aiming the gun with rock-steady hands.

She'd never killed anyone before, but hearing Gunner's pain, knowing Jim's monstrous nature. He deserved what came next.

A shot cracked through the office, deafening in the confined space. She twisted, staring at the man standing in the doorway, weapon raised. His shirt hung half-buttoned over jeans, his feet were bare, and for a moment she didn't recognize him. Then it registered—Rolf, almost unrecognizable out of uniform. His flat stare locked on Jim with the cold assessment of someone who'd seen evil before. But when he spoke to Nikki, his voice carried the calm authority she'd been correct to trust.

"It's okay, Nikki," Rolf said, weapon trained on Jim. "You can put away your gun. And call off your K9. We've got him."

CHAPTER THIRTY-ONE

Nikki sat in the passenger seat of Detective Mason's car, door open to the afternoon breeze, while he took her statement. Her throat throbbed where Jim's fingers had left painful bruising, but she'd refused transport to the hospital. Gunner sat beside her open door, watching the cluster of police vehicles that surrounded the office.

Through the doorway, she could see Jim's abandoned wheelchair. Crime scene techs worked around it, photographing and measuring, treating it like the prop it had been. She touched her neck, remembering his shocking speed, his fury.

"So after you discovered the crawl space, you called Lieutenant Decker?" The detective's pen moved steadily across his notebook.

"Yes. Put my phone on speaker and hid it under some files. Justin should have the whole recording."

"He does. Already sent it to us." Mason glanced up as a patrol car pulled away with Jim Turner slumped in the back seat.

"Between that and the rifle we found hidden in his van's compartment, Turner won't be walking, or wheeling, anywhere but prison. Although he will have his broken nose checked." The detective closed his notebook with a satisfied smile. "Rolf Olsen's statement tied it together. Says he was catching some sleep before his night shift when your K9 burst in. Grabbed his arm and wouldn't let go until he followed."

"That's not standard training," Nikki said, pride warming her voice. "He figured that out on his own."

"Smart dog." Mason smiled as Gunner's ears pricked. "Good timing too. Rolf said by the time he punched in the door code, you and Turner were in tight quarters with a handgun in play. That's why he fired the warning shot. So you wouldn't have to shoot."

Nikki nodded, hiding her jumbled emotions. She could still picture Jim exploding from his wheelchair. At that last second, she'd had her weapon aimed at his chest. She should have shot.

A paramedic approached, equipment bag in hand. "Need to check those throat injuries, ma'am."

"Please check my dog first. His ribs were slammed hard."

"I'm happy to do that." The smiling paramedic knelt beside Gunner, who suffered the exam with stoic dignity.

"No breaks," the paramedic said after gentle probing. "Just bruising. You've got a tough partner here."

"The toughest," Nikki agreed. Gunner's head lifted at her tone, his dark eyes reflecting absolute trust. She'd taught him to protect, to track, to find evidence. But today he'd done something beyond training. He'd recognized a deadly threat and sought help. He'd known exactly what she needed, as he always did. And luckily Rolf knew the code to that door.

The paramedic finished checking her throat, warning about potential complications and the need for x-rays. Nikki barely heard him. She opened and closed her fists, her mind circling back to how perfectly Jim had played them. His wheelchair, his strategic presence, his patient stalking of Kat.

She'd seen predators before, but few this calculating. To remain confined to a wheelchair for months, sacrificing his beloved trail rides and daily activities, all to create the perfect deception. His commitment to the fraud was almost as terrifying as his capacity for violence.

Her attention shifted to a car speeding into the lot—Justin. He opened his door and stalked toward them. Detective Mason took one look at his expression and stepped from the vehicle.

Justin slid into the driver's seat. "Got your evidence recorded. But, dammit, next time you decide to confront a murderous psycho, please wait for backup."

"Had the best backup right here," she said, touching Gunner's head. "Though I admit I didn't expect Jim to move that fast."

"Right." Justin's gaze pinned hers, his eyes reflecting a cop's dark experiences. "But to my ears, it sounded like you were trying to rile him. Like you wanted him to give you a reason."

"It's hard to remember exactly," she murmured. But they both knew what had driven her. The same rage that always surfaced whenever she encountered predators that targeted vulnerable youth.

"Nik." Justin's voice gentled though his eyes remained steely. "I understand. But going in there hoping he'd give you justification to shoot? That's not justice. That's vengeance."

"But he is guilty." She pressed her shoulders back against the seat. "And there might not have been enough evidence to convict. He really thought he could get Rachel back by killing Kat. And he was going to keep trying!"

"Delusional thinking. Common in stalking cases." Justin touched her shoulder, the gesture both a comfort and a warning. "The DA's adding attempted murder charges for you and Kat. Between that and Sophia's murder, Jim won't see freedom again. The system worked this time."

The unspoken words hung between them: Unlike with her sister's killer, who hadn't been caught in time. The system had worked now because she'd forced Jim's hand, made him show the monster hiding behind a wheelchair. She'd learned the hard way that sometimes you have to push predators into the open. And in that regard, she thought differently from Justin.

Following procedure, waiting for evidence while watching another young girl die—she couldn't live with that. However she pressed her lips together, keeping those thoughts to herself. Justin was a good detective who believed in the process. But sometimes justice needed a nudge, and waiting for the system to catch up often cost innocent lives. She'd known exactly what she'd been prepared to do. And she'd do it again to keep Kat safe.

It was a relief when movement near the office gave her an excuse to escape Justin's perceptive gaze and step from the car. Crime scene techs were carrying out boxes of documents and two computers.

She moved toward them, needing distance from this conversation, but could feel Justin following. Of course he wouldn't let this go. Not when it echoed his deepest fears about her PI work—that her emotions might override caution, that her determination might push her into situations where backup wasn't available. His concern wasn't only about today but about every future case where she'd make split-second decisions, with no one to pull her back from the edge.

But right now she couldn't face his judgment, not while her mind kept circling back to those months of Jim's deception. The way he'd watched Rachel while plotting against Kat. His terrifying patience that had almost succeeded.

"You saved the insurance company a bundle," Justin said, following her gaze on the techs and offering her a temporary reprieve. "Detective Mason says Jim admitted regaining mobility months ago but kept up the act. Sophia helped him, but became increasingly jealous of his feelings for Rachel." He paused, his voice thoughtful. "Jim claims Sophia's death was an accident, that Kat was the real target. But likely he was relieved to have Sophia gone."

He checked his phone, frowning at a new message. "They're digging into those medical reports now. One doctor's signature looks suspicious. Different from his standard documentation. Might be a forgery, or he was paid off. Either way, Jim had help maintaining the fraud."

"He was so obsessed with getting Rachel back," Nikki said, remembering the mutilated photo in Jim's desk. "When Wellington forced Conan out of Santa Anita, it played right into his hands. Rachel and Kat were back at his facility, close enough to watch, to manipulate, to target. No more driving across town for glimpses of Rachel. And he finally had a chance to eliminate what he saw as the only real obstacle."

"Speaking of Conan," Justin said, steering them both toward safer emotional ground. "The Derby's on Saturday. Think your client is still planning to run?"

"After everything Jim put them through?" Nikki felt a smile tug at the corners of her mouth. "Rachel and Kat won't let that man destroy their dreams. They've fought too hard to stop now. Besides, Conan has shown what he can do under pressure. He deserves his shot."

Gunner whined, his attention focused on a man emerging from the office. Rolf's shirt was now properly buttoned and tucked into his jeans, hiking boots replacing his bare feet. The canvas bag looped over his shoulder looked military issue, probably containing everything he valued.

"Nikki," he said, nodding respectfully at both her and Justin. "Just wanted to say—that's some dog you've got. Never saw anything like how he tracked me down. Left no doubt about what he wanted."

"He is special. And your timing coming through that door was pretty special too. Glad you knew the combo."

"Gunner was very insistent." A hint of humor touched Rolf's voice. "I wanted to keep sleeping, but he didn't give me much choice."

He extended his hand to shake Nikki's. "Won't be seeing you here again. The last thing Jim did before they put him in that squad car was fire me." Rolf seemed more amused than concerned, as if losing his job was a minor inconvenience compared to the satisfaction of stopping a killer.

"Jim's vindictiveness knows no bounds," Nikki said, watching Rolf stride toward the parking lot. Another casualty of Jim's obsession, though unlike Sophia, at least Rolf was walking away alive. "I should call Rachel, let her know what happened."

"Yes," Justin said. "She needs to hear it from you. You've been with her through this whole mess. Mason said they'll have the formal charges filed by tonight. Hopefully Rachel can focus on training, build up her race stable. With any luck, Jim will end up in maximum security, far away from her and Kat."

And far away from girls like Ashley Robart, Nikki thought, falling into step beside him. Gunner trotted ahead, tail held high, acting as if it had been another routine day. The late afternoon sun brushed the barns gold, making the training center look peaceful. Hard to believe these same buildings had concealed such malice.

But Saturday would bring a new chapter, one filled with thundering hooves and Derby dreams, instead of rifle scopes and obsession.

She just hoped Conan was ready to make history. For Rachel, who'd believed in him when no one else would. For Kat, who'd trusted him with her life. And for Marco, whose quiet devotion had never wavered through every threat and challenge.

They all deserved their moment in the winner's circle, this time with no one edited out of the photo.

CHAPTER THIRTY-TWO

Nikki sat at the railing of Justin's owner's box, breathing in the familiar race day atmosphere—freshly harrowed dirt, popcorn, spilled beer, and that distinctive mix of excitement and money. Below them, the crowd pulsed with movement while the bugler's call to post echoed across the grounds. Vendors shouted their wares, ice rattled in plastic cups, and the announcer's voice boomed over it all, creating that symphony of sound unique to racing's biggest moments.

Her throat still showed bruising but the physical effects of Jim's attack were fading faster than the memories. She pushed those thoughts away, choosing to focus on Rachel and Kat who sat beside her, their eyes locked on the track where the horses were appearing for the post parade.

"He looks calm," Kat said as Conan and his jockey, Elena, emerged from the tunnel, moving with contained energy beside his steady escort, Sugar. The two horses walked in tandem, looking as if they were old friends. Conan's coat gleamed dark against Sugar's lighter bay coat, but they matched stride for stride.

"Conan's mind is wonderfully clear now," Sonja said, her confidence steadying them all. "He understands exactly what's expected of him. Marco says he settled into his new stall like he'd lived there all his life."

They all glanced toward the finish line where Marco's head was barely visible among the crowd pressed against the rail. The white towel and halter looped over his shoulder served as a useful beacon.

"Conan expects his groom to be waiting at the finish line with his sponge bucket and cooler," Kat said. "So Marco insisted on watching from there. But we placed our bets together, even laid some exactors, on Sonja's advice. Apparently Sugar is very clear about who he thinks will run second."

Nikki laughed, feeling lighter than she had in weeks. Kat vibrated on her seat like any excited teenager, with no sign of her past wariness. And if she and Marco had taken Sonja's betting advice, there was a good chance they'd be walking away with money in their pockets.

The twelve-horse field paraded past the stands, greeted enthusiastically by the cheering crowd. Nikki couldn't help noting how Wellington's horse, Desert Warrior, reacted to the noise, rearing and fighting his escort. Already the colt's neck was streaked with white lather while Conan strutted like a seasoned performer.

The contrast was striking. Wellington's horse was burning precious energy, his nervous system flooded with adrenaline long before the starting gate even opened. And the fact that Conan and Desert Warrior had drawn side-by-side post positions seemed like racing's particular brand of irony.

"They're by the same sire," Rachel said, following Nikki's gaze. "He won the Saudi Arabia Gold Cup five years ago but he's known for passing on his hot temperament. Most of his offspring are talented though."

Nikki's chest flushed with unexpected pride, her fingers gripping the railing as the horses began their warm-up. Conan's mere presence in the race vindicated his connections' faith. Rachel's training methods—the taped crowd noise she'd played during workouts, the starter's bell recordings and the simulated race day chaos—had obviously prepared him well. He looked so composed, a three-year-old facing the roaring crowd, acting as if he'd been running in these big races for years.

"Ladies and gentlemen," the announcer's voice boomed across the track, cutting through the noise. "The horses are approaching the starting gate for the Grade One Santa Anita Derby, one of the most important Kentucky Derby preps. The winner today will earn one hundred qualifying points toward the first Saturday in May."

Justin appeared with fresh drinks, settling into his seat as the horses circled behind the steel starting gate. "How's our boy looking?"

"Perfect," Sonja said, though her fingers twisted the side of her flowing skirt. "But Wellington's horse next to him is a handful. He just wants to finish this and go back to his stall."

The horses began loading, one by one. Nikki felt Rachel tense as Conan approached the five hole. But he walked in, standing quietly while Elena gathered her reins. Three more horses disappeared into the gate. But one of the inside horses couldn't stand the wait and abruptly crashed through his door, leaving the crowd groaning.

"False start, number six Desert Warrior," the announcer said as a skilled outrider caught the agitated colt and quickly brought him under control.

"The horses will be unloaded while the vet examines Desert Warrior," Justin said. "Often it's safer to scratch."

"I hope Wellington's horse is okay," Rachel murmured. "But this delay isn't good for any of them. It's hard to switch off the adrenaline. "

But as the horses were backed out, Conan followed the gate assistant in a calm circle. Unlike some other colts that danced and kicked, he seemed unperturbed, as if the delay was just another training exercise.

"He'll be fine." Kat spoke with quiet assurance. "He learned to wait in those mountains."

The crowd's murmuring swelled as the vet completed his inspection. After a brief consultation with the starter, Desert Warrior was declared fit to race.

"Horses are reloading," the announcer said. One by one, the runners disappeared into the gate, each metallic clang of the doors ratcheting up the tension. Once again, Conan loaded like a seasoned professional, as if he'd done this a hundred times. Desert Warrior entered with less drama, though his tail swished in protest.

"All in," the announcer called. Nikki saw Kat's hand find her mother's, their fingers intertwining as if drawing strength from each other. For one heartbeat, perfect stillness descended over the crowd.

"They're off!" The gates swung open and Desert Warrior lunged to the left, slamming into Conan's shoulder. But Conan regained his balance and surged forward as Elena guided him clear of trouble. Within strides he settled into his fluid motion, running three wide when they pounded past the grandstand.

"Conan showing his tactical speed," the announcer said, his voice carrying over the thundering hooves. "Tracking the leaders into the clubhouse turn."

Nikki rose, her eyes pinned on Conan. Elena was sitting chilly, her hands quiet as Conan's stride ate up ground. Only one horse was in front of him, a flashy gray who was already digging deep, his head bobbing with effort.

"Look at him," Sonja breathed. "Conan's barely running." Rachel and Kat stood frozen beside her, their faces reflecting equal parts terror and hope. Nikki doubted they could even breathe, let alone speak.

The gray led the way down the backstretch. Conan closely tracked him, followed by a shifting herd of colorful silks. The gray's stride grew labored but Elena hadn't yet moved on Conan. He switched leads, perfectly balanced as they swept into the far turn.

"The leader drifting wide," the announcer called. "Conan and Elena Winters biding their time in second. Desert Warrior is making a gallant effort and is running third."

"Come on, boy," Kat whispered. "Show them what you can do."

As if feeling her encouragement, Conan's stride lengthened. Without visible effort, he drew alongside the tiring gray. His jockey's hands remained still, yet they were inhaling ground with every stride. The crowd's roar built to a crescendo as the horses straightened for home.

"And here comes Conan!" The announcer's voice lifted with excitement. "Taking command at the head of the lane. The gray dropping back as Midnight Flyer launches a bid on the outside. But look at Conan cruising on the lead. Elena Winters hasn't moved a muscle, maybe saving him for Kentucky!

"Conan by two lengths with a furlong to run!" The announcer could barely be heard over the crowd's thunder. "Desert Warrior has stalled but Midnight Flyer is closing the gap!"

Elena glanced beneath her arm, checking for challengers, then gave the slightest shake of the reins. Conan responded instantly, somehow finding another gear.

"Conan showing his class in the Santa Anita Derby!" The announcer matched the crowd's growing excitement. "Four lengths clear and widening with every stride! What a performance!"

Nikki jumped up and down as Conan approached the finish line, amazed Rachel could remain so composed. Even Justin vibrated with excitement while the announcer could barely contain himself.

"Conan dominating down the stretch!" the announcer said. "Five lengths clear under a hand ride! Elena Winters taking a peek back but no one's catching him today! And here comes Conan to win the Santa Anita Derby in spectacular fashion!"

Elena rose in the stirrups, one hand patting Conan's neck during the gallop out. The horse's stride remained powerful and steady, despite his performance. His fluid motion seemed almost casual, as if he'd been out for nothing more strenuous than a morning work at Mountain View.

The crowd's cheers greeted Elena as she guided Conan back toward the winner's circle. Other horses returned, blowing hard and lathered, but Conan still looked fresh.

"He did it!" Rachel's voice finally revealed her emotion. "He cruised around there. Even after everything."

Sonja nodded with silent vindication, the psychic who'd first understood Conan's strong personality. However her eyes gleamed suspiciously bright.

They rushed down the stairs, threading through the crowd toward the winner's circle. Nikki bumped into Rachel when the woman jerked to a stop, as if she wanted to absorb the scene: Marco beaming with pride, Kat hugging Conan's neck, Elena's smile radiant as she accepted congratulations.

This was what truly mattered, Nikki thought, not the claims of danger or the whispered doubts, but a horse and the miniscule team who'd never lost faith. The supposedly dangerous outlaw had shown his big heart, first in those treacherous mountains and now before thousands at the track.

Rachel glanced back, her eyes clear of past shadows. She gave Nikki a heartfelt hug then hurried forward to join her daughter and their remarkable horse.

CHAPTER THIRTY-THREE

A light breeze rippled over the flower beds as Nikki turned into Mountain View's parking lot. The center looked different now, peaceful and welcoming. Flowering jasmine had replaced the crime scene tape, and the office building had lost its sinister edge.

Gunner sat up straighter, his tail thumping with delight. Nikki glanced out the side window, surprised by his shift from alertness to anticipation.

"What is it, boy?" she asked, turning off the engine and following his gaze. Rolf stood at the side of the parking lot, nearly camouflaged against the grass, clipboard in hand. As usual, Gunner had recognized a friend before she did.

"There's our hero," Rolf called as Gunner jumped out and enthusiastically greeted the man, clearly remembering how Rolf had backed him up during the office confrontation three weeks ago.

"How's security duty treating you?" Nikki asked, noting Rolf's smile and relaxed stance. He seemed to be enjoying his new role as Conan's watchman.

"Best job I've had since leaving the service. Thanks for the recommendation." Rolf gestured toward the dirt path where two riders walked their horses toward the track. "Gets me outside, travelling to different tracks. And these people—they're good folk."

Nikki recognized Conan with Kat on his back, the big horse moving with his usual contained power. Beside them ambled a familiar looking Quarter Horse. Ashley had finally returned to riding, and Rachel had arranged for her to exercise Sonny, knowing the steady gelding would help rebuild her confidence. The girls' heads were tilted in conversation, neither noticing Nikki's arrival.

"Rachel's in the barn with Marco," Rolf said, shifting his clipboard. "Though fair warning, she has reporters camped around the grandstand. It's a zoo over there. She's meeting with them in half an hour. Everyone wants to know if the miracle horse is heading to Churchill."

"And?"

"She's letting Conan tell her." Rolf's smile held genuine appreciation. "Says there's no point having an animal psychic on speed dial if you don't listen to what the horse wants."

Nikki laughed, remembering Sonja's knowing looks whenever Conan was mentioned. Her friend had recognized from the start what everyone else had missed. Sometimes a horse's behavior wasn't about violence or rebellion. Sometimes they just needed extra time and understanding.

Rolf stepped away to direct a delivery truck backing toward the paddocks, its flatbed loaded with gleaming new portable panels, clear evidence that Mountain View's expansion was already underway.

Nikki headed into the barn, Gunner trotting beside her. The cool interior wrapped them in familiar stable quiet. Marco smiled a greeting then returned to filling Conan's double haynets. The everyday routines continued but the tension that had hung over the barn was gone.

"Nikki!" Rachel emerged from the tack room, envelope in hand and genuine warmth in her smile. "Perfect timing. I was just reviewing Conan's blood work. Come see what you think."

Carefree laughter drifted through the rear door, widening Rachel's smile. The sound of Kat and Ashley enjoying their morning ride spoke volumes. Some healing couldn't be measured in race results or purse money. Watching both girls recover their joy around horses seemed to mean more to Kat's mother than any Kentucky Derby opportunity.

"I can't thank you enough," Rachel said, holding out the envelope containing Nikki's payment. "Without you, this would have turned out much differently—though some strange things are still happening.

"Like Wellington suddenly wanting to send you horses?" Nikki asked. "Or the mysterious new owner of Mountain View?"

"You know about that?" Rachel's eyebrows lifted in surprise.

"Mike Jensen's latest blog post." Nikki pulled out her phone, navigating to The Racing Insider's website. "Take a look."

MOUNTAIN VIEW'S NEW CHAPTER by Mike Jensen

In a stunning development, Mountain View Training Center has been purchased by an undisclosed buyer who immediately named Rachel Parker as the head trainer. The prestigious facility, which made headlines with its Santa Anita Derby winner Conan, will undergo extensive renovations while maintaining current training operations. Even more unexpected is James Wellington III's announcement that he plans to send several promising two-year-olds to Parker for early conditioning.

"I admit I misjudged both horse and trainer," Wellington stated. "Rachel has shown exceptional ability with young horses. Her success with Conan proves she has a special touch with challenging

individuals. We're particularly interested in having her work with Desert Warrior and his gate issues before targeting the Belmont."

While Parker's training program expands, the question dominating racing circles remains: Will Conan contest the Kentucky Derby? The talented trainer is taking a thoughtful approach, putting her horse's wellbeing first.

"The Derby is incredibly demanding, especially for a horse who's already shown such courage through unprecedented challenges," Parker said in a recent interview. "While Conan has certainly earned his spot, we'll let him tell us if he's ready. There are plenty of prestigious races later in the year."

This reporter applauds such careful consideration. It's that kind of thoughtful horsemanship that's not only made Mountain View's new head trainer a rising star, but continues to change how the industry views both horses and trainers.

Rachel handed back the phone, visibly swallowing. "So we've gone from pariah to prodigy overnight. Hard to believe. Wellington actually called yesterday about Desert Warrior. Said he's been wrong about a lot of things."

"Including Conan the Barbarian?"

"Including that." Rachel's smile held both relief and pride. "Though I wish I knew who bought the facility. Even my attorney says it's all very confidential. But you want to know the weirdest thing? Jenny just received an official letter advising that Sonny would have free board here for the rest of his life."

Warmth spread through Nikki's chest as she considered the Saudi representatives who'd tried to buy Conan, and their unexpected sense of honor in leaving Sonny unharmed. "Sounds like the new owners really care about horses. And maybe felt sorry for Sonny's experience."

Rachel nodded slowly. "That's what I thought."

Their eyes met in mutual understanding, neither needing to say more. After all, some secrets were better left buried.

⸺●⸺

OTHER BOOKS BY BEV PETTERSEN

Jockeys and Jewels
Color My Horse
Fillies and Females
Thoroughbreds and Trailer Trash
Studs and Stilettos
Riding For Redemption
A Scandalous Husband
Backstretch Baby
Shadows of the Mountain
Along Came A Cowboy
Grave Instinct (Nikki Drake K9 Mystery)
Repent (Nikki Drake K9 Mystery)
Bone Trail (Nikki Drake K9 Mystery)
Dead Man's Trail (Nikki Drake K9 Mystery)
A Pony For Christmas (Novella)

About The Author

USA *Today Bestselling Author* Bev Pettersen is a three-time nominee in the National Readers Choice Award as well as the winner of many other international awards including the Reader Views Reviewer's Choice Award, Aspen Gold Reader's Choice Award, Write Touch Readers' Award, Kirkus Recommended Read, and a HOLT Medallion Award of Merit. She competed on the Alberta Thoroughbred race circuit and is an Equestrian Canada certified coach.

Bev lives in Nova Scotia with her family—humans and four-legged—and when she's not writing novels, she's riding. If you'd like to know about special offers or just want to say hi, please visit her at http://www.BevPettersen.com